GW00356931

The Wow Signal

To Dermot
with all good wishes

Patrick

Oct 2007

Previous Publications

Poetry
Breaking Hearts and Traffic Lights – Salmon Poetry, 2007
The New Pornography – Salmon Poetry, 1996
Jazztown – Raven Arts Press, 1991

Audio Play
Doctor Who: Fear of the Daleks – Big Finish, 2007

Short Film (screenplay)
Burning the Bed – Songway Films/Fantastic Films, 2003

The Wow Signal

Patrick Chapman

Patrick Chapman

Published by bluechrome publishing 2007

2 4 6 8 10 9 7 5 3 1

First published in Great Britain in 2007 by
bluechrome publishing
PO Box 109,
Portishead, Bristol. BS20 7ZJ

www.bluechrome.co.uk

A CIP catalogue record for this book is available from the British Library.

ISBN 978-1-904781-75-2

Printed by Biddles Ltd, King's Lynn, Norfolk

To Sarah

Acknowledgements

Thanks to the editors of the following, where some of these stories first appeared.

Argus, The Irish Times, The Moosehead Anthology X: Future Welcome (DC Books, Montreal, 2005), nthposition.com, Sex & Chocolate (Paycock Press, Washington DC, 2006), The Sunday Tribune – New Irish Writing, The Virtual Writer, WP Journal.

Contents

Burning The Bed

Later in the afternoon, Caroline and Stephen put the bed
out of the top floor window and burned it on the beach.
That morning, Stephen had cut it into pieces with the
handsaw. It had taken all of his will to do it, not because he
was weak, but because it sickened him to acknowledge
what this meant.

Before going up to the bedroom, they stopped in the
kitchen for some iced homemade lemonade that Caroline
had kept in the fridge for a couple of days. She stood in her
white cotton summer dress patterned with wild flowers, he
in his checked short-sleeved shirt and blue Wranglers.
They paused there, in the small space that separated them.
After a few minutes, in which they drank the lemonade and
stared wordlessly at each other, Stephen gave Caroline a
nod. They put down their glasses and walked up the stairs.
They went into the bedroom and looked at the bed they
had shared. It was in perhaps thirty pieces, in the middle of

the floor. Little trails of sawdust surrounded the bits. The headboard was cut in three. It was a plain rectangular frame which, whole, had spoken of their mutual liking for elegant simplicity but which, now, seemed so much firewood.

The legs were separated from the rest of the bed, broken and cast to the four corners of the room, like the legs of a beast that could no longer carry them, one that had collapsed under the weight of their accumulated bad dreams. The frame of the bed itself was cut, like the headboard, in pieces on the floor. Instead of metal springs, their bed had had wooden slats interwoven to provide support and flexibility.

When they used to sleep together on this bed, their bodies had made it creak. Making love, they would hear a sound that, in retrospect, had seemed to Stephen to be echoed in the rhythm of the saw.

The mattress was coil-sprung and sewn with diamond patterns. It was slouched against the wall, just inside the door, a rectangle of light from the window bisecting its form.

Caroline said, 'This is it,' and turned to him.

'Let's just get on with it,' Stephen said.

He was a stocky man with strong, hairy arms. *His short-sleeved shirt*, Caroline thought, *those arms around my shoulders, his little pot-belly in the small of my back...*

Stephen bent to the floor and picked up two pieces of the bed frame. He took them over to the window and threw them to the beach below. Caroline began to help him. She took a piece of the headboard and flung it out. It missed the gap in the window, bounced off the frame that was hanging open, but did not break any glass in the panes. The wood made a dull sound as it fell to the sand, throwing up a shower of the fine white powder.

They worked quietly, each taking bits of bed to the window, throwing them out and then walking out of the way to let the other do the same. After what seemed like half an hour, but was probably only fifteen minutes, the remains of the bed were lying in an untidy heap on the beach.

There was still sawdust on the floor. Stephen swept a small pile of it with his shoe, making a comet's-tail arc on the floorboards.

Caroline said, 'Did you ever think we'd do something like this?'

Stephen replied, 'Let's go down.'

Caroline shrugged and left the room. Stephen, despite what he had just said, stayed awhile, kicking the sawdust. He listened to Caroline's footsteps going down the stairs. She was leaving him. She had left him already. They did not need to talk to sort that out. They had decided.

After a moment he followed her down. She was already on the beach, beginning to pile the wood in a small hollow that she had made in the sand earlier. He stood on the verandah of the summer house, looking over her head, out to the Atlantic.

'Come on, give me a hand,' she said.

He started, then walked onto the sand and began to help her.

The light in the sky was bright, but not blue. The sunlight hitting the horses' heads on the water seemed to reflect back on the underbellies of clouds. The cries of the circling seagulls were like atonal music, its austerity undermined by the rushing of the waves against the shore. For a second, Stephen considered that they might actually be living inside a New-Age music video.

'I forgot the firelighters,' he said, as the two of them worked in concert to make what would become a fire.

'We don't need them yet,' said Caroline. 'Just let's get this thing built.'

They worked for a few minutes. The slats that had once supported their bodies they now made into a tent structure, a wigwam around which they arranged other, heavier wood. Stephen could feel an old back complaint acting up. He stood up when they were nearly done – only a few pieces of wood remained – and watched as Caroline took one of the last bits and put it on the small hill of wood.

She stood up and looked at him. 'Are you going to just stand there?'

'My back.'

'Fine. I'll do it.' She took the last two pieces and placed them on the structure. 'There.'

'Let's take a wander. There's nobody around.'

'Come on, then.'

They walked along the edge of the beach, with Stephen nearest the water. Once, they would have done this hand-in-hand. Now, their hands stiffly by their sides, each felt a new awkwardness at the thought of physical contact.

They had been married for two years and had been seeing each other for three before that. Their wedding day promises seemed hollow now. Apart from the burning bed and the other furniture, their worldly goods amounted to a few possessions in the summer house and the car, an old Volkswagen, parked on the hillock behind the beach.

'What are we going to do now?' Caroline asked. Stephen did not answer directly, but looked out to sea. All the way to vanishing point, he could see only the water and the sky. A faint smudge on the horizon suggested an island.

'Remember the first time we were here?' he said. 'You asked me if I loved you and I said yes.'

'How many times did I have to drag that information out of you?'

'I know.'

Seduced by talk of old times, Stephen attempted to brush his fingers lightly against Caroline's. She did not move away. Each of them wanted to make contact but neither knew how, or what the consequences would be. Now, after five years together, they were toying with holding hands.

Finally, it was Stephen who said, 'Hold my hand.' Caroline gripped his hand but did not look at him.

'What are we going to do?'

'Take the car back into town.'

'And then…?'

'We have to get away from here,' he said.

'We'll drive back into town, then I'll get the bus to Dublin. You can have the car.'

'Hold me, just the once.' Stephen stopped walking. Caroline, still holding his hand, went on a couple of paces. Wordlessly, she turned to him. He seemed lost, like a dog whose master was about to be put down. She took his shoulders and buried her head in his chest. 'Stephen,' she said.

They stood on the beach for several minutes. Stephen was focusing on this moment. Caroline could think of nothing but what had still to be done.

'What about a baby?' he asked as she raised her head and looked into his troubled face.

'Let's go back,' she said.

They walked to the house, listening to the waves and the gulls. When they reached it, she went into the kitchen and turned the radio on. It was tuned to a pop station playing hits of the 1980s.

Stephen went into the living room and got the firelighters from beside the fireplace, the only part of this house that had been made of stone.

'I'll get it started,' he called over the blare of the radio. Caroline was already out on the beach again, sitting down in her bare feet and summer dress. She had the matches.

'What if it doesn't take?' she said as he emerged from the house.

'It'll take.'

He bent down by the pile of wood and began to place all but one of the firelighters inside. Caroline handed him the matches. He lit the last firelighter and put this inside the pile of wood. It was going to be a slow burning.

'What time is it?' Caroline asked.

Stephen, still kneeling by the fire, looked at his watch: 'Twenty past four. It'll be bright for a while yet.'

He sat down beside her, looking at the fire. Smoke was rising. The first licks of flames were beginning to work on the wood of the bed.

'What about the mattress?' he asked.

Caroline said, 'We'll burn it later.'

'Later,' Stephen echoed.

There was too much heavy wood for the conflagration they had expected, at least for the moment. Stephen considered getting some petrol from the car.

'We'll have to deal with it sometime,' Caroline said. She did not mean the mattress. Staring at the fire, she wondered if, when it really got going, it would be noticed. Would a passing ship, though she could see none on the horizon, mistake it for a distress signal and send a boat out to the shore, rescuing this pair stranded on the western edge of Ireland?

'What if somebody comes? Aren't fires illegal?' asked Stephen.

'Let's not talk now,' Caroline said.

There was a momentary pause before Stephen said, 'I'll be kind of sad to say goodbye to this place.'

'Have we any beer left?'

Stephen said, 'A couple of cans in the fridge.'

'It's not that I don't love you…' Caroline said.

'I thought you didn't want to talk about this now.'

'Get the beers.'

Stephen stood up, went into the house and got the beers. When he returned, Caroline was crying softly to herself. He dropped the cans in the sand and put his arms around her shoulders. She shrugged him away.

'We have to try to move on,' she said.

Stephen picked up one of the beers and snapped the ring pull. Lager spurted all over his hand. 'Shit,' he said, as he licked his fingers. He handed the can to her and picked up the other for himself. She downed a long swallow of the effervescent liquid; and made a whiskey face, even though she was drinking beer. She said, 'I suppose we could try again, in a few months.'

'What?'

'Let's see how we feel then, OK?'

'I thought you wanted out.'

They fell silent for a while, watching the fire build its cathedral of flames and smoke. It was still bright, but evening would not be long in making the sky greyer and the sea more mysterious.

'Remember the time in the pub, was it Hanlon's? We had just met and…' Stephen began.

'Don't start.'

'You were wearing a long black coat and nothing under it.'

'You enjoyed that,' she said, 'just knowing.'

'Everybody else in the pub, it was heaving, everybody else in the pub was getting twisted. Summer. The whole place was throbbing with sex. Seemed no-one was actually getting laid, though, except us. There they were. A hundred people getting shitfaced, hoping they'd end up with someone at the end of the night. And all the time, we knew.'

'We had just fucked,' Caroline allowed herself to join in his reminiscence. 'You were feeling all smug.'

'Lucky bastard, that was me.' Stephen put down his beer. 'Listen, I'm going for a swim.'

'You shouldn't swim with drink taken.'

'See you later.'

He walked to the edge of the water, took his shoes off and started to paddle in the incoming waves.

'The tide will get your clothes,' Caroline called after him, but he didn't look back. Stephen took off his shirt and threw it on the beach. Then he rolled his jeans off, revealing his white legs and backside. His arms were tanned up to where the shirt had covered them. The tan on his face and neck stopped at the collar. Like a man committing suicide, he walked into the water. It was

17

freezing. He allowed himself to walk in up to his waist, then lie back, letting the water carry him. Maybe, he thought, it would take him all the way to America. He closed his eyes, his body bobbing up and down in the sea. Then, he turned himself on a gentle roll of surf and began to swim out. Stephen had a sense of the depth beneath him. The alien worlds below. If he dived deep enough, he might mutate into a form of life that could survive the pressure, the non-human environment. He might lose the anthropocentric world-view he had always accused others of but had rarely suspected in himself. He thought himself not only aware of the other life forms on Earth, but also of how small this world had really become. Although he now felt at one with the sea, he was also aware of the reality. He was an interloper.

Stephen stopped swimming. On a whim, he let the water take him under and then, he felt the beginning of a pain in his torso. Through the wall of sea, he could see Caroline approaching the edge of the land, a water-mirage. The sea drew him down again.

Rallying his energy, he tried to swim to shore. His head turning from side to side, he caught glimpses of Caroline through the water. She was walking into the sea. She was reaching out to him. As he approached the shore, about to black out, he could not tell how near he was to safety, or how close he was to drowning. Disabused now of his romantic notion of being one with the creatures of the deep, Stephen swallowed water.

Then, in an instant, Caroline pulled him out of the waves and dragged him onto the sand.

She was frantic. She knelt down and started to give him mouth-to-mouth. She pummelled his chest with her fists.

He spluttered: 'I'm all right!' But she did not seem to hear him. She was in floods of tears. She grabbed him by the shoulders and shook. When he looked up, he could see that she was distracted with fear.

'I thought you were gone,' she said. 'I thought I'd lost you.'

Stephen let her collapse on top of him. He held her in his arms. They were both confused. They lay like that for a long time. He could feel the tide lapping at his bare feet as if the sea had unfinished business with him and was summoning him back. He held her closer than he had in a long time. Her heart beat against his chest. But it was no good. They had burned the bed. How could there be any coming back from that?

Stephen tried to comfort her. Quieter now, she seemed slightly embarrassed at her display of emotion. 'It's all right,' he said. 'I'll live.'

When she drew herself away from him and stood up, he could see the silhouette of her body through the material of her dress and found himself confused by desire.

She walked away, picked up his clothes and his shoes. She dropped them in a bundle beside him. 'I'm sorry,' she said.

'I'm fucking sorry too,' Stephen replied, raising himself from the sand.

Caroline went back into the house. Stephen stood awhile, looking out to sea. There came the silver body of a naval rescue helicopter, the sun glinting off its rotor-blades, whose sound followed them like a coda. It was flying low over the hills to the east, moving inland, oblivious to these two people and their little fire.

The blaze that they had made of the bed was going well now. Stephen felt the heat on his face. Smoke rose in the late afternoon air, like the ghost of their relationship, climbing into the sky that ended in the darkness of space.

Happy Hour

They are sitting in the chrome-fluorescent limbo of a fast-food place called Charlie's. It is an October Saturday, just after three in the afternoon.

Father and daughter. She is having a Charlie Burger and Coke with fries. Against his better judgment, he is having Charlie Chicken Nuggets and a Sprite.

It is always visiting time at Charlie's. Fathers are there with their daughters, or their sons, over in Kiddies Korner, all brightly painted walls with murals of animals and characters from Disney films. There's Pocahontas. Over there is Hercules. Just to the left of him is The Hunchback of Notre Dame. It's like a crêche with cholesterol.

'Your mum still singing opera?' asks the dad, Howard, forty next birthday, successful accountant and failed husband. Receding grey hair longer at the back than front, aquiline nose, clear blue eyes surrounded by crows' feet. Laughter lines. Mouth full of nicotine-yellowed teeth. He is wearing jeans and a denim jacket over a black t-shirt. He thinks that his clothes make him look younger than he really is.

'Aieee-dah!' exclaims Beverly, his daughter, going on eleven. Blonde hair in pigtails. Fresh pixie face. She is wearing a purple top and red jeans, both presents from him.

For almost a decade, Beverly has been led to believe that singing opera is what mothers do when they wish to express themselves. They burst into song. Great, whooping arias. Mumma sings in the shower, *Raindrops Keep Falling On My Head* to the tune of *Ode to Joy*.

Howard daydreams:

'Mumma, does Daddy sing at work?'

'I expect he does,' Mother trills, not in song, but in a sing-song voice.

Beverly imagines her father breaking out *Sweet Charity* to the monotonous clacking of keyboard keys. 'Jesus, if my friends could see me now.'

Back to reality.

'What's the latest on Bill?' Howard asks. Bill is the new boyfriend of ex-wife, Marian. Bill is an electrician; though he seems to spend most of his time in the house, reading *The Sun*, drinking beer, watching television. Freelance Electrical Consultant.

'I think they're going to get married,' Beverly says.

Howard is silent for a while. He has barely touched his Charlie's Chicken Nuggets.

'Still drinking?'

'He comes over sometimes and shouts and Mumma starts singing. In the bedroom.'

'Right effing madhouse,' Howard mutters.

'You shouldn't swear in front of the children,' Beverly smiles, indicating with the sweep of a French fry the kiddies in the Kiddies Korner.

Howard knows how things could turn out if Bev were to take sides against him. *He was swearing*, he suspects, is a phrase that, in the wrong mouth, could be transformed into *He was using abusive language*. Hey presto: no visiting rights.

'So does he come home drunk often?'

'A couple of times a week.'

'Is he OK with you?'

'He brings me presents. You know the Playstation I wanted?'

How can he explain that the other man, this usurper, is trying to buy her affections?

Wondering where Bill had got the money, but assuming that electrician's work, like plumbing, pays well, Howard asks, 'Playstation? What does it do?'

'You plug it in and you shoot things.'

'You shoot things?'

'Like bad aliens and Imperial Stormtroopers. I'm Lara Croft sometimes and sometimes I'm Princess Leia.'

'Least you're not playing with dolls.' Howard takes a sip of his Sprite.

'Mumma says they're bad for me. I'll grow up submissive.'

Howard nearly chokes on his drink. 'Where did you learn to pronounce a word like that?'

'Mumma.'

'Does her singing bother you?'

'It's very loud. She does it at night too when she can't sleep and Bill is in the bedroom with her.'

Howard's stomach leaps into his chest at the thought of his ex-wife in bed with Bill. Springs coiled and registering each shock of orgasm like a Richter scale. Like a bloody earthquake in Tokyo. It is the same bed that Howard and Marian used to share, for Godsake.

'Do you ever see them?'

'No,' Bev says. 'I'm usually fast asleep like a good girl.'

'How's school?'

'Sokay.'

'Are you learning anything?'

'Yesterday, Teacher lined us all up in a line and told us to name birds. I said Pterodactyl. Teacher said don't be stuuuuuupid.'

'Your teacher's wrong,' Howard says. *The kid has imagination,* he tells himself. *That teacher shouldn't be discouraging it.*

'She said a pterodactyl is extinct so it doesn't count. But when Billy Mears said Dodo, she said Good Boy. I just don't get it, Daddy.'

'You watch out for that teacher. They don't have all the answers. Your burger all right?'

'Yeah. It's nice. But you know what I'd really really like next time, Daddy?'

'What's that, Bev?'

'I'd really love a Strawberry Charlie Shake. Big Cup with three straws. One for me, one for you and one for Sandra.'

'Hmmm.' An imaginary friend.

'If I promise to be good during the week, will you get me one next time?'

Howard smiles, charmed by his daughter's tactics. 'You can have one now, if you want,' he says.

'CanICanICanI?'

'I'll just go and get it.'

'ThankyouThankyouThankyou.' Beverly jumps up and down in her plastic seat.

'Don't get too excited. It's only a milkshake.'

'But it means you love me, don't you Daddy?'

'Yes, I do,' Howard says, getting up to go to the corner. 'Strawberry?'

'That is co-rrect!' Beverly says, mimicking her teacher.

'Back in a minute.'

It's a short walk to the counter, behind which Charlie's Elves, as the employees are officially known, are cooking meat, toasting burger buns and pitta bread, chopping vegetables, stirring cold sauces.

There is a queue three-deep. Howard is used to this. Every Saturday in the year since the settlement of his divorce from Marian, he has brought his daughter here. It isn't lack of imagination that prevents him from taking her to galleries, kids' movies, funfairs in the summer, ice-skating in the winter. It's Marian's insistence that these are places where they are likely to linger. One hour a week. That's their allotted time. Just enough to get a burger and have a chat, what Beverly calls her regular debriefing. Howard is proud to be reminded every week of just how bright his daughter is for her age.

'One Strawberry Charlie Shake, Big Cup,' he says, when his turn comes. It strikes him as ridiculous that marketing has reduced common transactions to baby-speak. If you try to say Strawberry Shake instead of Strawberry Charlie Shake, the Elf will correct you.

'One Big Cup Strawberry Charlie Shake coming up, sir.'

These people are too damned perky, Howard thinks.

While he waits for the shake, he reminisces about his divorce. There had been nothing particularly wrong with the marriage, according to the law. Just because people didn't get on after twelve years, it didn't mean that they had to get a divorce. So, despite his and Marian's intention to do it cleanly, quickly, and with as little hurt as possible, the lawyers had said that there hadn't seemed to be grounds. To get it over with, he had had to sign a statement admitting to having been a bad husband and father, neglectful of his daughter and cold towards her mother. He had had to paint himself in such an unfavourable light, in fact, that Marian had found herself taking advantage of his signed statements to get custody. Whereas they had begun proceedings on cordial terms, by the end of the whole process, they had been hardly speaking to each other. Marian got Beverly. Howard was demonised by the judge as unfeeling, irresponsible and just short of dangerous. One hour a week access. Half of his monthly pay cheque in alimony. He lives alone now, in a bedsit.

But this is his hour. The Elf brings the milkshake and Howard returns to the plastic table at which Beverly is arranging her French fries into a face.

'Here you go, princess,' Howard says, handing her the Strawberry Charlie Shake.

'Thanks, Daddy,' she says, absentmindedly, as though she no longer wants it. Howard watches her putting a moustache of half a fry on the face she is making.

'It's Bill,' she says.

'What?' Hackles raised.

'It's Bill,' she repeats.

'What has he done?'

'Silly Daddy. He hasn't done anything. The face is Bill. He has a moustache.'

'Listen, Bev,' he says, 'will you look at me when I'm talking to you?'

Beverly looks up. She does not like the tone of his voice.

'It hurts me when you talk about Bill. Could we not talk about him, please?'

His daughter understands. She nods sternly. Then she wipes the French-fried face on to the floor.

Howard is immediately repentant. 'Oh, sweetheart, I'm sorry. I didn't mean to upset you.'

'It's all right, Daddy,' says Beverly.

'Come here,' he says. He reaches over to her to give her a hug but as he does so, he knocks over the milkshake. The plastic cap comes off and pink goo pours out on to the formica.

'Daddy!' Beverly jumps back, avoiding the goo.

'Shit.' Howard stops in mid-embrace.

'Swearing!'

Howard sits down, finds a paper napkin under Beverly's carton of fries and starts to mop up the mess. He looks around for some Elves to help him, but can't see any.

'My Strawberry Charlie Shake is ruined!' Beverly says in mock reproach, laughing and clapping her hands. 'Did you get any on you, Daddy?'

Relieved that she is not angry with him, Howard finishes mopping the shake. The napkin is inadequate. He has the milky stuff all over his hands.

'My trousers,' he says, wiping his hands on the thighs of his jeans.

Beverly giggles. 'You can use the dry cleaners, can't you?'

'Sure can. Listen, Bev, I'm sorry about what I said about Bill. I shouldn't've. It really is none of my business what your mother does or who she does it with.'

'DaddyDaddyDaddy,' Beverly tries to interject.

'Sorry. What you want to say?'

'Daddy,' Bev reassures him. 'It's OK. I understand.'

'No, I mean it. You can mention him all you like. Otherwise I might get into trouble.'

'What kind of trouble, Daddy?'

'Well,' Howard hesitates. 'You know.'

Beverly doesn't know. Her burger, though getting cold, is still edible, untouched by the spill. She finishes it, munching.

Just like a munchkin, Howard thinks.

'You're a munchkin,' he says to her.

Mouth full of burger, Beverly asks, 'Daddy, what's a munchkin?'

'*Wizard of Oz*. Or is it *Willy Wonka*?'

'That's the umpahs, Daddy. Can I be Dorothy instead? I don't like munchkins.'

'All right,' Howard says. 'You can be Dorothy.'

'And if I click my heels can I come live with you?'

Howard says nothing, but looks down at his empty hands, crossed on the table.

'Can I be the Good Witch of the East?'

'You can be Toto if you want,' Howard says.

'Can I finish your Chicken Nuggets?' Bev asks.

'Go ahead,' Howard says.

She picks them out of his carton, one by one, biting each of them in two and chewing each half meticulously.

'You're supposed to chew nine hundred and fifty-seven times each time you eat something,' Beverly says.

'Only munchkins do that,' Howard tells her. 'Little girls don't have to.'

'Good,' Beverly continues to eat. 'Then I won't.'

Howard looks at his watch. It is nearly ten to four. They will have to go soon.

Just then, his mobile phone starts to vibrate in the breast pocket of his jacket. It's Bill, calling as he does every Saturday, to remind Howard that his time with Beverly is almost up. As he does every Saturday, Howard lets the phone vibrate. Bill will leave a message, which Howard will delete. It has occurred to him to leave the phone behind when he is seeing his daughter, but the call is now part of the ritual. Howard wonders if Marian knows what Bill does. Maybe she encourages him to do it.

'Daddy, your phone is having a heart attack,' Beverly says before the phone stops vibrating.

'Who taught you about heart attacks?' he wonders.

'Bill. He also says I'm adopted. Am I, Daddy?'

Furious at Bill, Howard grits his teeth. 'No, you're not. Bill has no right to say that. He's a fucking layabout –'

'Language.'

'Sorry, sweetheart.' Howard puts his head in his hands. 'I'm sorry.'

'It's nearly four,' says Beverly, sadly. A few of the other customers have looked over to see what is happening but, engrossed in their own mini-dramas, they soon turn away.

'Daddy,' Beverly says. 'I know I'm not adopted.'

Howard looks up. He puts a hand out. Beverly takes it. She seems more grown up than he is.

'Time to go,' Howard says, standing up, breaking the link. 'I have to get you back to County Lock-Up before four o'clock or my privileges will be rescinded.'

'What's "rescinded"?' Beverly asks as she, too, stands up and pulls on her little green jacket. It makes for quite a clash of colours.

'Taken away,' Howard explains. 'Let's get the hell outa Dodge.'

Beverly does not hold his hand. They walk to the door. She says: 'Shouldn't we put the rubbish in the rubbish bin?'

'That's what the Elves are for,' he says. 'Anyway, it wasn't fast and it isn't food.'

'Don't be silly,' she says. 'I like Charlie Burgers.'

'You won't when you grow up...' he mutters as they walk outside into the wind.

Wet leaves have been plastered on the pavement since this morning. Dry ones are blowing around in flocks, as though they are alive and autonomous. Howard likes autumn. But now, as he accompanies Beverly to Charlie's

Car Park, he feels the wind in his bones. Winter is coming on, taking out its thermometer and plunging it in ice.

'I'm getting old,' he says as they reach the car, a four-year-old Volvo that Howard had bought with her protection in mind.

'Old man,' Beverly jokes. 'My Daddy is an old man.'

'That's enough out of you,' he says.

They get in.

'Seat belt,' Howard says.

'Daddy,' Beverly asks as she straps herself in, 'am I really adopted?'

'Listen,' he says, turning the key. He has forgotten to do up his own seat belt. 'If Bill tells you that again, I'll go over there and wring his neck.'

'Reeeally?' she asks, teasing him.

He puts his foot down and drives off. It is only a few minutes to the house, fifty-two doors up Lavender Terrace.

Howard stays quiet on the way. Out of the car park, through Main Street, cutting through a yellow box just as the lights change to red. Two roundabouts, half a mile along the motorway to the suburbs, then down an exit to the terrace. It is an old development. Marian and Howard had lived in number fifty-two for five years. There are still nineteen years left on the mortgage.

Howard knows that Marian will be waiting on the doorstep. His beautiful, bitter former wife who has come to believe the statements he had signed in order to get them a painless divorce. She does not seem to remember the man she had married. Kind, witty, playful. At one time or another, she has described him as being all of those things. Now she considers him a threat to her new stability, as she calls it.

The car pulls up at the kerb. As expected, Marian is on the doorstep. Howard keeps the engine running.

'See you next week, Daddy,' Beverly says, offering her cheek with a squint of her left eye.

'See you, sweetheart,' Howard says and kisses her goodbye. He tries not to catch Marian's stare as he reaches over to the door and opens it for his daughter. She gets out, closes the car door and waves to him. Then she turns, opens the front gate, skips through and up the path to her waiting mother. As Howard drives away, Marian throws her arms open to collect her daughter and lift her into the air as though delivering her from an unnameable menace.

A Ghost

A story in the area had it that a murderer once lived in the house the man was watching and that nowadays, if you waited up long enough, say until three in the morning, you could hear his footsteps dragging along the floorboards. You could feel the air disturbed by his passing, a current brushing your cheek. In a small town where people are suspicious, where people are superstitious, a house like that could go untenanted for months or even years. Still, until recently, a woman had lived there, and a man had watched.

There was a time, soon after she had gone, when the man wondered why the woman had moved out. He thought sometimes that perhaps she had detected his presence. Had she caught him in a shaft of moonlight as he watched, thinking himself to be unobserved?

For months, she had seemed almost to provoke his interest, his dogged and regular observation. At precisely eight-thirty every morning, he would see her draw back the curtains of the upstairs right-hand window, and she would be wearing a dressing gown, loose, exposing her breasts for a fleeting moment. He would wait the twenty minutes or so until she had finished her shower and her morning routine, hoping to catch sight of her naked body as she dressed for the day. Then, realising that he was late for work, he would quickly put on his own clothes and dash out the door, regretful, and, on the way to his job in the fish factory on the outskirts of the town, he would cast a quick glance up at her window to find her dressed, taunting him.

All day long as he took his knife to the cold and slippery bodies of tuna, he would think of her. He did not know her name or where she came from, because, like many a man before him, he kept much to himself and did not participate in the town gossip. He wondered if anyone was watching him? Could passers-by see the sliver of his body that was revealed in the parting of the curtains that he hid behind as he stared at the woman across the road?

He knew from hearing distant snatches of her voice that she was an American, come to spend a little time in the town, but for what purpose, he could not say. At night, when he got in from the factory, he would undress, have a shower and fantasise about being watched. As the water in its halting cataract bombarded his goosepimpled body, he would think of the woman and imagine her eye at the other side of the shower curtain, looking at his body in a strange negative of his own eye at the curtain where he watched.

Did she go to a job? Did she get home from hers before he got home from his? He would get out of the shower and, the towel around his shoulders, his neat hair dripping water into the cloth, he would stand once more behind the curtain and watch. He spent many evenings like this. At six-thirty, after his shower, he would begin the night vigil, often spending several hours just watching, even if he could see nothing.

He would set his alarm clock for seven-thirty, to get in an hour's watching in the mornings, before she pulled back the curtains. He thought to himself: *I am making a film. The retina is my camera.* Like the making of any film, this one too entailed a lot of waiting around before anyone got down to any acting. Most nights, he waited until she went to bed before he himself retired. In bed, he edited his film. The long waits were cut. The camera of his own eye turned in imagination into an endless zoom that gave him a disconcerting feeling of weightlessness — zooming in on a subject that was moving away at the same rate of speed.

The woman performed for him a seemingly endless loop of the same actions. Opening the curtain, vanishing behind a door into the bathroom, emerging fully dressed or sometimes half-dressed but less inviting. He could not remember the details of her body. In his fantasy, she appeared somewhat as an indistinct figure, as though she represented for him all the women of the world.

One day in the fish factory, at the height of a summer heatwave, the man began to think about the murderer. In 1946 there had been a killing in the town. A young woman had been found beside a stream in the woods, her throat cut. She had been heavily pregnant. Police suspected foul play and went after the man who lived in the house across the street, a bachelor in his thirties who was known to have courted the woman and who the town grapevine had down as the father of her unborn child. When the body was found, the police called on the man at his place of work, the local newspaper office where he was a typesetter. The man protested his innocence but had no alibi and was taken into custody. He was found guilty of the crime and hanged. The house, which had been left to him in the will of an uncle, lay empty for years until it was bought from his estate by a developer who refurbished it and put it on the market. A family from out of town, blow-ins, moved into the house. Twenty years later, they moved out. A succession of short-term tenants followed, each apparently scared off by the dragging foot of the murderer's ghost.

Finally, last summer, the American woman had arrived, unpacked her suitcase and had taken up residence. Perhaps she was searching for her roots, or writing a book about murderers. Maybe she was simply a rich woman on her own seeking the quiet of a small town.

The man began to notice her movements and set his life in motion to their regularity. The woman became his clock. Through autumn and into winter he watched, as the trees outside his own house grew bare, uncovered by the frost. The icy air cut him to the bone as he walked to work, casting his customary glance at her window. November passed into December and as Christmas approached, the first snows began to land softly on the road and the rooftops, only to dissipate in a day. The week before Christmas, a heavy fall arrived, dusting the landscape with a coat that revealed his tracks like an elemental policeman taking fingerprints. He trudged to work every morning, leaving his tracks in the mantle of hard snow. Every evening on his way home, he noticed these earlier prints heading towards him. He felt like a man walking through the body of his own ghost.

He spent Christmas alone in front of the television; he was an only child and his parents had long since passed away. They had left him the house, this red-bricked terraced two-storey place that was merely a link in the long chain that formed his side of the street.

The woman had gone away for Christmas, probably to her people in the Bronx or South Central, or wherever she hailed from, some amorphous melting pot that welcomed back its diaspora on special occasions. He noticed her absence on Christmas Eve. On holiday from work, he had gone back to bed after the alarm clock ring, relying on his established pattern to alert him at eight-thirty. It was unusual that he should forgo his morning vigil but it was Christmas Eve and he had decided to allow himself a lie in. When he finally went to the window he saw no sign of the woman. Her curtains were closed. Early morning frost webbed the panes. The street, never normally busy, was now completely deserted. In an hour, perhaps, last-minute shoppers would begin day-long foraging excursions through the town in search of tinsel, wrapping paper, turkeys that they had saved coupons for with their local grocer. There was a Protestant grocer and a Catholic grocer in the town, just as there was a pharmacy, a bank, a network of pubs and a butcher's shop for each denomination.

His unwelcome Christmas surprise disappointed; but, in the manner of the meek, he soon resigned himself to the fact that she was gone for the holiday and he would have to wait perhaps a week for her return. That day, he made no attempt to enter into the festive spirit. He was known in the factory as a quiet sort, a man of few words and fewer opinions. In fact, as he gutted and cleaned the fish day-in, day-out, he seemed almost a part of the conveyor belt, another link in the mechanism. The knife was an extension of his personality. When, on Friday evenings, the day shift ended and the workers went to the pub, he rarely joined them. Indeed, he had been toying with the idea of acquiring a Pioneer pin in order to pre-empt any invitation to be sociable. He had stopped going to Mass, so that he could spend more time at the window. Now that the woman was gone for Christmas, he played with the possibility of attending the service in the morning. *But*, he reasoned, *what if she is sick? What if she has not gone away and is simply indisposed? Will she be back tomorrow?*

On Christmas morning, the television was starting up its programme of religious ceremonies. At the usual time, he was at the window, awaiting the coming of his own particular saviour, the woman. She had continued, for months now, to be the protagonist in his nightly film. What was he going to do if the star did not appear? He would have to rely on the footage already shot in his mind.

That morning, when she failed to throw open the curtains, the man lingered a while at the window, behind his own curtain, and watched the space where she should have been. In his reverie, her body now took on his imaginings of an ideal figure behind that tantalising dressing gown. He remembered her as someone perfect.

St. Stephen's Day followed without her, as did the next day and the next and all the days that came one after another like frames of blank film stock that was running out of the projector into the air, planting empty images on the molecules that he breathed. He saw her mirage everywhere. In the New Year, he reasoned, she would return. He resolved that when she did, he would never let her go.

January arrived. There was no woman. A 'to let' sign which some mischievous child had changed with a felt-tipped pen to 'toilet' appeared in the window where the woman used to be. He was beginning to remember her in more vivid colours, as though his film were showing on an unbalanced television. Each morning he woke at seven-thirty, earlier than before, keeping watch, oblivious to the sign. Each evening he spent many hours looking for her in the same place and finding nothing but her absence. By the second week of January, it occurred to him that he had not returned to work and that the doorbell-ringing he had heard two days in a row, earlier in the week, had gone unanswered like the post in the hallway.

He set up a camp in the bedroom. It was like a fallout shelter. All of his food, all of the tins and packets that had been in the cupboard downstairs, and all of the comestibles he had bought in the local shops, spreading his purchases among them so that he would not arouse suspicion, he now ranked by the skirting board beside the wardrobe. He had a plate and a knife and a fork, a tin-opener and a spoon. He drank lead-tainted water from the rusty faucet in the bathroom. He watched for the woman into February, into March. He ignored the doorbell, kept the television on, the radio tuned to a talk station. He was growing thin.

Late in March, he decided to open his post. There was a letter from the factory enquiring as to his whereabouts. There were bills from the electric company, the gas company, the cable company: threats that he would soon be cut off. There was a demand from the landlady for two months' rent; his standing order had lapsed with the discontinuation of his pay cheque and the dwindling of the money in his bank account. He was now overdrawn, said a bank statement. There was a letter from a woman, a stranger from America, saying hello.

He took this letter upstairs, reading as he mounted the creaking steps, and entered the bedroom.

I knew you were watching me, said the letter. *I saw you watching me.*

It was the woman. It was the woman. But he did not know her, this woman who had written to him, amused and slightly admonitory. His actress had not gone away, he saw then, for as he wandered towards the curtain, he could detect movement in the window across the street. So he put the letter from this impostor under his mattress and continued to watch.

***

Days go by. He spends weeks in front of the window. His beard grows long. His fingernails arc out, becoming claws, like those of a guitarist renouncing his talent. The food in the cans is nearly gone.

The man watches. Now, he sees the woman every morning and every evening and for several hours in the gathering darkness. He sees her as he waits behind his window, his empty eyes staring past the sign at curtains that never open.

And as delirium comes upon him, he remembers.

He remembers himself as he was, one moment years before, prone in the woods by the stream, a foetus growing inside him and the woman from across the street standing over him, with a fish-gutting knife in her hand.

Venus d'Arc

My eye, at last. For the first time, I can see. There is a background in place, to give me a context. Some buildings, some water, a little vegetation. It is still all very rheumy and insubstantial, but it is all that there is, for the moment. However, now, I have sight. My swirling iris holding in place a surrealist cornea: there is no optic nerve behind it, but the fact of the painted eye is enough.

He continues to make more of me. I am getting an eyelid but no brows: how strange. There is a veil, a light covering over my head. I am wearing clothing peculiar to this time: fifteen hundred and something, perhaps.

He is standing there in his smock, palette in one hand, brush in the other. He frowns as he leans over to me and applies more skin. I do not know what to say. Should I be grateful to him for giving life to me?

I wonder at my sex. Glancing down, I see that I am female. That means that the model who is posing for this artist is also female. Is she simpering in his presence? The great artist who commands the affections of women everywhere. The bearded ruffian who eats too much, who drinks too much, who shouts too much. I expect that soon, I will be privy to their world, mute witness to what goes on in the studio.

***

He showed me his ornithopter today. He means to fly through the air on this screw. It looks like a screw to me, a screw with blades. The passenger stands inside the frame of the mechanism, turns it with a handle and the blades rotate, scooping up the air and thereby allowing flight. It is fascinating but, if he wants to get to a far-off place, why does he not just paint it?

It appears that he does not respect his model, the one who is posing for me. After he has shown me his design, he calls her a dimwit who does not understand him, who would not know a piece of art if it were to smack her in the face with a lick of paint. He says that this painting would have more appreciation of his work: hence his helicopter revelations to me. Does he know that I am conscious? If only he had drawn my lips I could go *brrrrrr!* like the blades of his machine and prove it to him. But I am yet without a mouth, ears or a nose. He has not drawn them yet.

At least I will not catch a cold.

Later, they make love: my creator and my model. He throws her to the ground and rips her undergarments away, lustily, then tells her how lucky she is to be fucked by him. She responds, somewhat angrily, that she always imagined that little boys were more his thing. He strikes her, tells her not to make him angry or it will go the worse for her.

***

As part of his ongoing renovations, the artist has installed a mirror on the wall, by chance, opposite me. It allows me to see myself. It turns out that I am not a face of any kind that you might expect. I am a clock-face with one bright eye in the middle, between the butts of the two hands frozen in time upon the physical frame of a human face. In other words, I am a human with a clock for a face. I had been hoping that he had made me into another Giaconda, another Mona Lisa, after the great Leonardo, whom he idolises. But no. I am a clock-face with one eye on a human body *dressed* as Mona Lisa. Complicating my identity crisis further, I have overheard him calling me *Temporal Venus*. I do not rate his originality.

***

Discovery time. As the first drop of paint hit the canvas to make me, I became aware of a greater world, stretching back into the past and forward into the future. It turns out that paintings, like humans, have race memory. I recall the original Mona Lisa. She was pretty for her time and inscrutable for eternity. I find myself on speaking terms with Picasso's weeping woman, Munch's screaming figure, Botticelli's Graces. I am also aware of art-ghosts such as Van Gogh's severed ear. Spooky. This ear, though not in the picture, is implied by its absence. It exists in Art Limbo, a state of non-being for everything that does not appear in art but can be inferred from a viewing. At least that's how I explain it to myself.

My mind has bathed in the water of Monet, roasted in the hells of Bosch, floundered on the wreck of the Medusa. I have squared up to Mondriaan, bounced with the basketballs of Koons, pixellated inside a Pollock. All art is related in this way, has instant access to everything ever painted, sculpted or installed.

***

The model asks him what art is. He has no answer. She should ask me and I will tell her that art is nothing and everything; it is the most important thing in the world and the most useless; it is life and it is death.

Not only humans make art. Have you ever experienced the ramblings of roaches, the doodlings of dogs, the watercolours of whales? Well, obviously not. But there are animals who make art. Sometimes, and don't ask me to explain this, because you wouldn't understand – sometimes there is art that makes animals.

For a painting, consciousness comes as something of a sensual rush.

I am hung up to dry in the artist's studio while he makes love with the model again. But what has happened to her? This morning, they spent some hours writhing on the floor in front of me and I saw her face. It is the same as my own. She is literally my model.

Hello, Cyclock.

***

She has gone shopping for him. Bread. Milk. Grenades. *Grenades?* He has arranged these items on a table and begun to paint them, together with a skewered, cooked rat. It is a meaningless tableau: two grenades between which is laid a French loaf. The rat kebab is a little to the rear of this construction; the milk forms a spill-lake between the grenades, their pins still in place. He takes red paint on his brush and he flecks it into the milk. He is going to call it *Blood Bridge.*

Meanwhile, I dry.

It does not seem to take him long to forget me. He has not looked at me since the last brushstroke painted the hour, four o'clock, on my face. Time, for me, stands still at four.

And the model? She is nearly always naked now, her clock-face as immobile and impassive as my own. There is not so much as a tick out of it. I have still not discovered the artist's name; I remain unsigned.

***

She has been for plastic surgery.

Months have gone by. It is the same model because he uses the same name to address her. *Whore.*

Now her face is different. The clock hands have been removed. The huge, central eye has been replaced by two small ones on either side of a fairly ordinary nose.

Where her mouth should be, is a cavity that goes all the way through. There is a dove in the cavity, behind a metal grille that starts under her nose and ends at her chin. The model is a walking birdcage.

He wants her to pose for him again. She refuses, telling him that she is still recovering from the surgery. She will be his lover, she says, but she will no longer be his art-whore. He strikes her, bursts his knuckles open on the cage, cries out in anger and sucks the blood from his hands. He mutters something about the rarity of female reproductive juices being used as paint in pictures. He yells out for the ghost of Helen Chadwick to inspire him, but she is not in. The model cries out, too, through a small slit in her chin beneath the birdcage; perhaps this is her mouth.

I have no such opening.

You will be my model or I'll kill the bird, he tells her.

***

The artist has gone out to buy steak and shoelaces and a bottle of whiskey. The model comes over to see me.

Alone in the studio, she declares herself unhappy with the man who has immortalised her former image yet treats the living her with such contempt. I admire her as she addresses me. She says that she hates me, then she spits. I am offended but incapable of responding. Now, she takes out a knife and slashes me. I feel no pain, but am aware of the gash across my clock-face. She walks away. Through either side of the gash, I admire her posterior. It is shaped like the seat of a chair.

***

They argue again. He is shouting at her for having destroyed his best painting. I am flattered. His other works have garnered considerable acclaim throughout the art world. Even some members of the public have heard of them.

Somehow, he has tied her up, strapped her to a post that helps keep the ceiling up.

Her dove is dead of a knife in the brain. The hilt sticks out between the bars of the birdcage.

I do not know what to do other than to hang here, still drying but defiled. I do not care what they do with me but I hate being in a room when people are having a row.

It seems that the hands on my face now read five o'clock, but this may be the result of the tear.

He turns away from her and yells at me. He intends to burn me, for he can not leave a ruined painting in the agony of desecration. And as for her, the model: she has broken his heart. She will pose for him one last time.

***

He has detached her arms just above the elbows; the bandages are new. He has planted her up to the knees in a block of wet concrete. A metal frame holds her in the pose of Venus de Milo. She is drugged and unconscious and the gate of her birdcage hangs open and down like a useless metal tongue.

He stands at a canvas on an easel, painting her, bandages and all.

Flames lick the studio but he paints on, uncaring. He will kill us all.

As he paints her, I feel forgotten. Is it my imagination, or are the hands of the clock on my face spinning around insanely like the blades of an ornithopter?

I had thought that I was his Venus. His *Temporal Venus*.

But no. She is the one. It was always her. My model.

As the artist paints his Venus, born in flames, he does not even turn to see my face.

My ugly face.

My ugly face is melting.

The Worm

On one of her visits to his Dublin flat, his mother told Stanley about the night her brother died. They were on their second bottle of wine and the Eurovision Song Contest was drawing to a close on television. For once, Ireland was not winning.

Stanley's flat was warm. He and his mother sat at either end of his long couch, strangely comfortable with each other. He did not often see her. Being too busy with his job, he rarely ventured out of the city. Now, they had been talking over the sound of the television for a couple of hours, as though it hadn't been months since they had last met.

'He was very peaceful,' she said. 'You could sense the Spirit moving in that room. The nurse left me with Philip and Olivia and the kids, and, I'm not joking, but he looked like a man who was ready. They say that when your time comes, you see the angels gathering around your bed.

Anyway, and this is not a word of a lie, at the last moment, Philip looked around the room and smiled at me and then Olivia and then the kids. Like he was saying goodbye. Like his worldly troubles were over, thank God, and now he was going up to be with his wife, Joan.'

Stanley was shifting uncomfortably where he sat. He was not used to face-to-face encounters with such unshakeable belief. He loved his mother, certainly, but sometimes he found her religious conviction hard to take. She had a kind of born-again oneness with the universe, coupled with a conservative stance on private morality, yet she was one of the most laid-back people he knew.

She continued: 'There was a light, as if the ceiling was opening up for him, and he was ready to be lifted out of his bed. You could see he wasn't coming back. But his eyes were full of grace. After he turned to us and smiled, he lifted his face up to heaven and gave a little nod, as if he knew. And then, the nurse came back in. She was shaken, the room was so different. The presence was in it.

'Then Philip slipped away. I went over and closed his eyes. They were clear as day and he was still smiling. I'll never forget it.'

Stanley was in charge of the wine. He said nothing, but let his mother's mind take her back to the night her brother had died. He lifted the bottle of Shiraz, felt the weight and poured an extra-large measure for her, a little for himself.

She was smiling at him now, as though she had knowledge that he did not even know existed. He sipped his wine. His uncle had died nine months earlier. Stanley, on one of his rare trips west, had attended the funeral.

The conversation moved on to other topics: there was a powerful faith healer in Cavan; Stanley's father's arthritis was at him bad; the man who lived across the road had a new satellite dish, though he'd never worked a day in his life…

A couple of glasses later, Stanley saw that the wine had run out. His mother insisted on sleeping on the couch, so he brought the spare quilt out of the hot press and said good night.

Then he took himself off to bed where he slept the sleep of the drunk.

At work, the telephone rang. It was his mother.

'Stanley. I want to ask you to do something for me. Now I can't stay on the phone long, but it's this. Philip is sick in the Mater and I wondered if you'd go to see him for me. I can't get off work until Tuesday.'

'Do you want me to tell him anything?'

'No, I'll phone. But it'd be good for him to have the company.'

'OK, I'll see him on Saturday. I'll call you.'

'Thanks, son. When are you coming down?'

Saturday afternoon, Stanley took the number ten bus to Phibsboro and got off at the crossroads. It was a warm day. The place was its usual, buzzing, Saturday self. The carpet wholesaler's giant warehouse stood out garishly beside the downmarket ice rink, across the road from Sir Arthur Conan Doyle's. In a newsagent's shop, Stanley bought a few magazines, some Marlboro Lights, some chocolate and nuts. He did the lottery, although he was not in the habit. He tossed twenty pence to a man on the street; he regarded charity as a karmic protection racket and he gave when he thought that he might need good luck.

Stanley walked the hundred yards to the hospital. On the way, he remembered all the places he had lived in around here. A seventh-storey plasterboard apartment at Cross Guns Quay, near the shopping centre. A terraced house on Manor street, close to the Phoenix Park. A three-room flat above a dentist's practice on the New Cabra Road. All three had been burgled, prompting him to leave each time. He lived in Ranelagh now, with its gridlock and its sometimes boisterous nightlife.

At the reception desk in the Mater Hospital, he gave his name and that of the patient he wanted to visit. The receptionist told him to go to St Luke's ward, room nine. Stanley walked off in search of his uncle.

When he reached the ward, he waited by the enquiries desk. It took several minutes for anyone to attend to him. This place was quieter than he imagined. His only recent experience of hospitals had been as an outpatient in

Accident and Emergency in the Meath: he had endured long hours of boredom while he had waited for someone to see to a fractured finger; he had thought himself to be the calm centre of a storm of activity, although he had actually been irrelevant until his name had been called.

A short, energetic nurse arrived at the enquiries desk. She was obviously pressed for time, but took the trouble to inform him that his uncle was in room nine. 'Here,' she said in a Cork accent, 'I'll take you.'

His uncle was not there. Instead, Stanley saw a couple of old people watching television. There was some horse-racing from Cheltenham on the BBC.

Down the ward, a small, balding man in a dressing gown and pyjamas was walking slowly towards the telephone on the wall. The nurse spotted him.

'Mr Forrest,' she said, pointing, and then she was gone about other business.

Stanley walked towards the shuffling man. Could this be his uncle? Stanley had not seen him more than three times in his life. As he approached him, he said 'Philip?'

The man turned. He seemed confused, as if he did not recognise his visitor.

'I'm Stanley, Susan's son.'

Philip had telephone change in his hand. He looked at the coins, then at his nephew. A weak smile. He put the money into his pyjama jacket pocket then stiffly, he shook Stanley's hand. 'How are you?' he asked.

'I'm fine,' Stanley said. 'I've come to visit you, see how you're getting on.'

'I'll be right as rain,' Philip said. He was in his fifties but appeared at least ten years older. 'Come in and we'll have a chat.' As if he were inviting Stanley into his house, Philip took him by the shoulder and led him to the common room, two doors down.

Stanley said, 'Susan's asking for you. She's going to come as soon as she can get off work. You doing all right?' As they went through the door of the common room, Stanley observed that his uncle's skin was jaundiced. His eyes were sunken and his mouth turned down. Stanley did not know if this was how he had always been, or if illness had taken an especially heavy toll.

They sat down on two plastic chairs, facing each other. Across the room, a family visiting an elderly woman sat watching *Star Trek* on Sky One.

'I brought you some things,' Stanley said, stalling. He opened the plastic bag and took out the magazines: *Empire*, *The Phoenix*, *Vanity Fair*. Then he produced the chocolate, the nuts and the cigarettes.

'Well, thanks, but I'll only take the smokes. They don't like you smoking. That nurse is a fierce one for the smoking. But, as the man says, what's the harm now?'

Stanley handed over the Marlboros, put the magazines and the sweets back in the bag.

'They say the worst of it is over,' Philip said. 'I have an operation on Tuesday, so we'll see. I'll be out by Friday. Do you want to see my scar? It's a good one.'

With a smile, Philip bent down, rolled up the left leg of his pyjamas. A recent scar ran the length of his calf. Freshly stapled. Stanley did not know what to say.

'Isn't that something?' Philip asked.

'It is,' Stanley said.

'Are you the youngest?'

'I am.'

'And how old are you now?'

'Twenty four.'

'Are you working?'

'Yeah. In one of the studios here. I'm an engineer.'

'That's a good job.' Philip approved. 'There's money in that. Building going on everywhere.'

'I record radio. Commercials.'

The older man shifted in his seat. He took a packet of Major cigarettes and a purple plastic lighter from his breast pocket, then lit up. Stanley did not know where Philip had put the new box of cigarettes. 'Will you have one?'

'No, I'll have one of these.' Stanley lit a Marlboro Light.

'The nurse doesn't like me smoking,' Philip said. He took a long drag from his cigarette. For a little while, neither of them spoke. The clock on the wall said ten past three. Stanley had been in the hospital all of twenty minutes. Already he was in a curious state of alarm. There was no doubt that the uncle was on his way out. It was in his face, literally, in the yellow pallor that gave him the air of a man with one foot in the grave. His eyes were mischievous, as though he had seen it all, yet had not seen everything.

Philip finished his cigarette, dropped it to the linoleum floor, crushed it with the heel of his slippers. He lit another one, sucked.

'I remember you now,' he said.

'Oh?' Stanley said.

'You were only a boy when myself and Joan moved away to the Smoke. You were a bright one then. Singing for your grandmother. That tape is still there.'

Stanley did not know where to look. His grandmother had had a bright orange tape recorder, kept over from the Sixties, all curves. He had once sung a song for her. Something from the Glam Rock era. He had forgotten the incident until now and the memory of it unsettled him.

He was silent as Philip continued, puffing on his cigarette. 'And there was the time you were five and you and that little Russell girl from Ballyvaughan brought that farmer the milk. Fresh from the cow, still steaming. You carried the bucket between you. He gave you a shilling for your trouble. You slept in her parents' farmhouse that night, in the bedroom with the Dalek book on the shelf and the *Doctor Who* bedspread on the bed.'

Stanley was staring him straight in the eye, but it was as if Philip could not see him, almost as if he were in another place, another time. He threw the butt of his cigarette to the ground.

'She told you there was a barrel in the yard that would fill with water when it rained. Her sister nearly drowned in it. She showed you the barrel, then the two of you played on the swings on the little hill behind the house. If you fell off, she said, you could bang your head, do fierce damage altogether.'

'You can't know that,' Stanley said, quietly, but his uncle did not seem to hear.

'Remember the time you sat on your front porch. Summer of seventy six, it was. Hottest ever. You sat reading the paper with your aunt, Jim's sister, who was wearing a yellow suit with bell-bottoms. Great clothes they had them days. You're only three, but you ask her why that "i" in the newspaper is upside down. She tells you it's an exclamation mark.'

Stanley lit another Marlboro, dragged hard.

'And the time you stole a box of corn flakes from the grocer because you needed the cardboard to draw on.'

'How are they treating you in here?' asked Stanley. 'Is the food all right?'

'It's grand,' said Philip, throwing his cigarette to the ground, squashing it under his slippers. 'But you'd miss home cooking. Do you remember the earthworm?'

I don't believe this, thought Stanley. He began to fidget, taking his cigarette out of his mouth, putting it back in, dragging.

'Five years old. You had a bright red plastic tractor for riding on the footpath. Big black wheels. You in your little boy's bob haircut and the face of an angel. The sun was splitting the concrete. You saw an earthworm moving on the path and you decided to run it over. Not for any reason other than you wanted to find out what made it move.'

The family across the room seemed engrossed in the exploits of Captain Kirk. Stanley looked at Philip as if he were a madman. They had hardly talked at all about his illness. What was it he had? Stanley couldn't think of the name, but as Philip continued, he began to make a mental list of diseases and afflictions. *Acquired Immune Deficiency Syndrome. Bubonic Plague. Cholera. Dysentery. Emphysema.*

'So you ran that worm over in your tractor and saw what was inside. It was white stuff came out. And what did you feel?'

Halitosis. Irritable Bowel Syndrome. Jaundice.

'I —'

'You felt curious. Not sick, not upset, just curious, detached. You watched the two parts of the worm for a long time, after you drove your tractor over it again. You didn't know that the parts would grow back into two new worms. No idea about death yet, but you knew you were on to something.'

'How do you know all this, uncle?' Stanley asked, finally, putting his cigarette out on the floor.

'I know things,' Philip said.

Stanley was confused. He had been a teenager before he'd met his uncle for the first time.

'And I'll tell you what else I know,' said Philip, 'you never lost that.'

'Lost what?'

'The attitude, man. In college, you treated your boyfriends with the same detached curiosity as you treated that earthworm.'

'What do you mean?' Stanley was angry now but felt unable to rebuke a dying man. He put his Marlboros in his pocket, with the intention of leaving soon.

'That's another story,' Philip said, shaking his head, 'you know yourself. Don't mind me, I'm only an old bollocks. The noggin isn't as good as it was. Will you have one of these?' He put a Major in his mouth, offered one to his nephew. Stanley took it. It was more pungent than the Marlboros. He associated Majors with yellowed, stubby fingers, dirty nails. Philip lit both cigarettes.

'Now, tell your mother I was asking for her,' Philip said. 'I'll see her when she comes up. And you mind yourself. You're a good man, all the same.'

Stanley pulled on his cigarette, anxious to be away. 'Is there anything I can get you?'

'Do you have change for the phone? I have to call Olivia. And would you do something for me? Could you phone Jim Forde?' A local politician and noted puller of strokes.

'I'll do that.' Stanley handed over a few pound coins for the phone, despite remembering that his uncle already had change.

'He's in Leinster House. Owes me for a good few votes. He'll get me a medical card.'

'You've no insurance?' Stanley said.

'Where would I get the money for that? Call Forde and he'll see me right. Tell him I'll be in the ward until Friday but not to phone during the operation on Tuesday, because I might not be able to take his call.'

'I'll call him on Monday,' Stanley promised. 'He's probably away for the weekend.'

'Thanks for doing that for me.'

They sat in silence for a few more minutes. Philip adjusted his posture, then got up and said, 'I'll call Olivia now.'

Stanley followed him out of the room. They walked down the corridor to the telephone. Philip shook his hand. 'Thanks for coming to see me. Tell Susan I was asking for her.'

Then he turned to the telephone, giving it all of his attention as though he had already forgotten that his nephew had ever been here. Stanley walked away, without the plastic bag of magazines and sweets. Down the corridor, as he left the ward, he could hear Philip beginning an argument with Olivia, who had been his girlfriend since shortly after Joan, his first wife, had died of breast cancer.

Five days later, as he was waiting for a recording session to begin, Stanley decided to call his mother. But when he lifted the handset to dial, she was already on the line. Something funny with the electrics, he decided.

'Come down for the funeral,' she said. Stanley remembered then that he had neglected to telephone the politician.

That evening, he took a train. During the three-hour journey, he wondered how his uncle had known so much. Who could have told him about the earthworm?

Later, when he asked his mother if Philip had ever mentioned him, she said that no, he hadn't been in the house except for one Christmas when Stanley had been a teenager and one Easter some years later. He'd had his own family to raise.

In the funeral parlour for the removal, Stanley saw his uncle for the last time. His body was smaller now, as though the life essence, in leaving him, had taken some of his stature with it. Philip's body, in the coffin, was like an approximation of the man Stanley had met at the hospital.

His mother was inconsolable as Philip was put in the earth. Hard spring rain needled the gathered mourners.

The day after the burial, Stanley took the train back to Dublin. He did not speak with his mother about her dead brother again until the night she came to visit.

In the months that followed, he saw an earthworm only once. It was in the garden of a house in Ranelagh that he passed every day on the way to work. Now, one Tuesday morning in late summer, the worm caught his attention.

Traffic was gridlocked on the Appian Way, the delay caused by two number 18 buses stopped side by side near Leeson Street. Other people were walking to their offices: women wearing blue jackets and skirts above white trainers; men in nondescript business suits, some wearing large headphones over their ears. Stanley caught the sound of mid-period Phil Collins emptying out of someone's head. But here was a worm, more fascinating to him now than his usual pastime of people-watching.

Stanley stopped, bent down and peered through the railings at the little creature. He understood the need for worms, but found it difficult to empathise with them. Now he wondered if that worm in the garden was newly sprung, or if it had grown from one half of a body cut in two.

The Electrical Store

On his summer break from school that year, William got a job in Mr Severin's newsagent shop on Seaview's main street. He had not wanted to work, but his mother had convinced him that the money would come in handy.

'Think of all the things you can buy,' she had said. 'You can get shoes. You can buy yourself some new clothes, instead of relying on us all the time, and look how you're shooting up: you'll be taller than your father soon. You can get your own school books next term. You can even pay your own way into the disco and buy your own drink.'

This last suggestion was not meant in earnest. William had just turned twelve and he did not go to discos, let alone drink alcohol. In fact, he hardly knew what a girl was.

It was true that the money would come in handy. He had his eye on a few albums in the local electrical store that also sold records. He wanted the *Saturday Night Fever* soundtrack, with its fabulous gatefold sleeve and its combined twenty-four-inch-diameter vinyl. William dared not calculate the circumferences of both records. He also wanted the Kate Bush LP, *The Kick Inside*, because her voice was so unusual and the sleeve intrigued him: Kate holding on to the crossbar of a kite that seemed to be flying into the eye of a giant. She was wearing a long red dress and she had flowers in her hair. There was oriental lettering down the right-hand side of the sleeve. The third record William had to get was the Sex Pistols album, not because he liked the music, but because the other kids in the school seemed to think it was cool to wear safety pins in their t-shirts. William thought that it just looked grubby.

However, he would have to wait for the records he really wanted. The owner of the shop, Mr Smythe, made monthly trips up to Dublin. If William took the job, he could order the albums. Then, Mr Smythe would collect them in the city and William would listen in secret to the music he had previously heard only on the transistor radio, under the bedclothes: Mozart, Mahler, Bach. The adults did not seem to approve of children listening to classical music but William had a feeling that Mr Smythe would understand the strange desire of a boy stranded in a small country town to escape through both headphones at once. William would have to ask Mr Smythe not to let the other kids know about the classical discs. But first, the boy had to go to work. The job was just the thing. Besides, the newsagent was across the road from the electrical store, so he could keep an eye on the window where albums were displayed, alongside various labour-saving devices for the home.

William turned up for work at eight in the morning of the first Saturday in July. He was wearing the clothes that he usually wore when he had to appear neat. Grey shorts with one pocket on the right-hand side. Orange-and-brown-striped tank top. His shirt was grey, to go with the shorts, and was open at the neck, the collar spread out over the shoulders of the tank top. His shoes were copper brown, with a punched-hole pattern on the toes. His blond hair, parted in the middle, went straight down below the nape of his neck. It often got in his eyes.

He reintroduced himself to Mr Severin, the shop-owner with whom his mother had arranged the job. The old man did not seem as severe as his name might suggest. He greeted William affably, asked him if he would like a cup of tea before they started, said he was about to have one himself. There were Marietta biscuits to be had, too.

William drank tea with his new boss as they stood by the counter and exchanged small talk. Mr Severin was a grey-haired bachelor in his early forties. People said he was funny, but he looked serious enough to William. He wore a waistcoat of pinstriped black cloth in front and red silk at the back. A white shirt under this, a purple bow tie, hand-knotted, and grey wool trousers atop black, meticulously polished patent leather shoes, gave him a resemblance to a bank teller that William had seen on *The High Chaparral*. All he was missing were the arm grips and the green shade over his eyes. Mr Severin already had the appropriate side burns, shaved to a point, as though they were suspending his mouth between them.

The shop was small but brightly lit with fluorescent bulbs in the ceiling. In the front was the counter with its chiming cash register. William liked the sound it made and the way the price flags popped up in the window. This Sale...K-Ching! These days, the prices were in decimal.

On a rack opposite the cash register, just inside the front door, there were stacks of newspapers. The *Press*, the *Times* and the *Indo* would be waiting in tied bundles every morning, out on the pavement, said Mr Severin. William would have to take them in and place them on the floor beside the front counter; although, this morning, the old man had done it himself. There was not much demand for the *Times*, because this was mostly an *Independent* town. Every week, the local paper, *The Seaview Register*, would be delivered by a grumpy man on a red-and-white scooter. There were still two copies of last week's edition left.

Down the back of the shop, beside a secondary counter that was smaller than the one up front, another rack displayed the periodicals. *The People's Friend, St Martin's Magazine, The RTE Guide* and, curiously, old paperback pulp magazines from ten years before: *The Man From U.N.C.L.E. Magazine, Argus, Amazing Stories*. Their covers had faded and the pages had gone brown.

There were also comics on this rack, few of which William still sneaked a look at. *Bunty, Mandy, Warlord.* In his mind, there was essentially little to distinguish between Misty and Union Jack Jackson. They just used different weapons.

A new comic had become popular recently: *2000AD.* It cost 8p in Earth Money and William could see that it was available on Neptune, a snip at 8g. He liked Dan Dare the best, then M.A.C.H. 1, and Judge Dredd, but, caring little for sport, he was not so keen on the Harlem Heroes or Claw Carver.

Mr Severin said that a lad like him should have grown out of comics by now, but what did he know? He was in his forties, after all. They probably hadn't even had comics when he was a boy.

In the middle of the shop was a free-standing unit that offered stationery: airmail writing pads on whose covers there was a line-drawing of an air hostess in a pillbox hat and a tiny – but probably ginormous in real life – aeroplane flying through clouds, leaving a pen-and-ink slipstream. You could also get brown envelopes, black marker pens, red biros, Helix rulers, set squares and callipers. Books of tickets for raffles, bingo or checking coats in the community centre. Lined copy-books. Grid-lined maths books. Musical notation paper, bundled in quires.

Apart from the pulp magazines, there didn't seem to be any books with actual words in them. William reflected that there were no bookshops in the town. In the local library, you'd be lucky to get anything more challenging than Mills and Boon or Louis L'Amour. You might occasionally find a couple of *Perry Rhodans* (of which there were already ninety-two), but William preferred the Ray Bradbury and Thomas M. Disch books that his aunt smuggled to him by post from Manchester where she lived. *102 H-Bombs*. Now there was a book.

Behind the counter, on a high shelf, stood plastic jars of sweets, all dusted and sticky inside. Aniseed balls, jelly babies, gob stoppers. Liquorice sticks, tangled red and black, Torpedoes which would lose their colour in seconds, Kola Kubes that always seemed too acid to the taste, once the sugar coating had dissolved. There was a weighing scales on the counter with a small tower of weights standing beside it, in eighths, quarters, halves and a full pound. A little stack of brown paper bags and a scoop sat beside the weights.

William's first day began with the newspapers. Mr Severin gave him a few tasks to get him started and explained in detail what the boy had to do. While his boss guarded the till, William took the bundles of papers to the counter at the back, cut open the plastic wire that bound them and counted out the copies. Sixty-five of the *Independent*, thirty-five of the *Press* and only twelve of the *Times*, half of which were on standing order. William noted these amounts in a ledger, then put the papers on the rack in the front. As per instructions, he kept six copies of the

Times back and wrote on each the name of a different customer. Then he gave these to Mr Severin who put them behind the front counter for the customers to collect.

As the hours passed, William observed the clientele. Mostly old men, it seemed. A balding, raincoat-wearing gentleman who was hard of hearing, came in at around eleven. He was Mr Samson, retired from an occupation that William could only guess at. He began a conversation with Mr Severin by ordering his usual forty Senior Service cigarettes: two blue packets that spoke of a superior smoke and a discerning smoker.

Later in the morning, William had to wash the floors. Mr Severin gave him a large bucket, a bottle of pungent cleaning fluid and a mop that was almost as tall as himself. The boy did not like the sound of this job.

'Start at the back,' Mr Severin had told him, 'and work your way to the front. Don't let any customers slip.'

William began by taking the bucket to the kitchen in Mr Severin's flat above the shop and filling it with hot water from the tap. He came downstairs and started on the floor. As he mopped, Mr Severin dealt with the customers.

Mr Cohen came into the shop. He was a superannuated tailor with a stooped gait, who now spent his days roaming the town, chatting to everyone and anyone.

'Get stuck talking to him,' William's mother had often said, 'and you'll never escape.'

To William, he seemed harmless enough. Mr Cohen was one of the six who reserved the *Times*. He did not stay long after he had bought the paper and did not actually say much at all. But after he had gone, Mr Severin said, 'I thought I'd never get rid of him.'

It took William half an hour to do the whole floor. In that time, three other customers came in.

Amos Johnson, a young man who walked with the aid of two sticks, came in for plug tobacco and insisted on filling his pipe there and then, talking to Mr Severin as he did so. Pipe lit, Johnson was off.

After he had gone, Mr Severin said, 'Nothing wrong with that fecker. Disabled, my arse. I'd give my right arm for his cheque every week.' He did not seem to realise what he had said.

O'Brien, a returned Yank who had been in Korea, wandered in for gum drops.

'Sweet tooth,' he explained to Mr Severin.

The shopkeeper, filling out a quarter on the weighing scales and tipping the sweets into a bag, joked, 'Lucky you have any teeth at all. The sugar in them things will rot the ones you've left. That'll be forty-five pence.'

Baker, the local charity fundraiser, came in collecting for some Asian famine that William was not familiar with, even though it was probably on the news every night. Mr Severin sent him away without a penny.

'Come back when you want to buy something.'

The old man seemed to like his job. It appeared to William that he enjoyed passing remarks on the customers who were his livelihood.

The boy spent the rest of the morning tidying shelves, taking longer than was necessary, in order that the work should fill the time. Every so often, he would stare out of the shop window at the electrical store across the road. At lunchtime, he would go over there and find out how much he would have to save to get the records he wanted.

The clock over the front counter clicked to one p.m. Mr Severin asked William to look after the shop while he went upstairs for potted meat sandwiches and tea. 'Back in an hour,' he said.

The hour was a long time passing. William dutifully guarded the till, standing behind the register, flicking through this week's *Warlord*. Lord Peter Flint was single-handedly fighting Germans who, as they died, were ejaculating strange terms such as *Schweinhund* and *Aaaarrrrgh!*

He looked at the clock. It was two p.m. Mr Severin would be down any minute now and William could go across the road.

He imagined the scene. 'Excuse me, Mr Smythe,' he would say politely, 'but how much is the boxed set of Pablo Casals playing the six Bach cello suites? And what do I need for Mozart's *Symphony No. 40, K. 550*, performed by the Academy of St Martin in the Fields? Or what does it cost for the new Abbado recording of Mahler's *Second*?'

Mr Smythe would be unable, no doubt, to give him a price straight away. 'I'll order them for you, if you like,' he would say. 'I see you've got a job across the road. Five pounds a week? Well, I suppose you'll have saved up enough by the time I make my next journey to Dublin. There, no sooner said than done. Your name is?'

'William, sir.'

'All right, William, is there anything else I can do for you?'

William would ask him to set aside the *Saturday Night Fever* soundtrack and the Kate Bush album. He would pay him at the end of the week and collect the records. 'Five pounds should be enough?' The Sex Pistols could wait.

Mr Smythe would probably warn him about spending too much, too soon. 'The pleasures of hearing Casals playing Bach's six cello suites, which I, myself, have done often, far outshine those of Ms Bush's voice which, I'll allow, is an extraordinary instrument to be in the possession of a popular singer.'

William knew as he saw the clock hand moving to a quarter past two that he had been daydreaming again. Where was Mr Severin? Those potted meat sandwiches must be something special.

At the risk of leaving the cash register unattended, William decided to go upstairs and get his boss. Lunch hour was only an hour after all, even for employers. And besides, he was starving.

He walked over to the door, flipped the sign so that it said Closed, and went to the door at the back of the shop that led upstairs.

'Mr Severin!' he called out. 'It's nearly twenty past two!' He expected Mr Severin to shout that he would be down in a minute. But there was no sound from upstairs. Could he be asleep?

William took a chance. He climbed the short staircase to the flat above.

'Mr Severin!' he said at the top of the stairs. There was still no response. He went into the kitchen and there he saw Mr Severin at the table, slumped over, face down in a bowl of leek and potato soup, cold now, filmy about the old man's sideburns and the bridge of his nose.

William's blood froze. There were lunch things scattered on the tablecloth. A pint of milk had spilled over the bread and the sliced, gelatinous Spam. Mr Severin was out for the count, and no mistake.

The boy walked over to his boss and shook him by the shoulders. Mr Severin would not wake. Some soup had spilled out of the bowl and over the rim of the table into Mr Severin's lap.

William did not know what to do. He tried to raise his boss again and rest him against the back of the chair, but it was no good. He had to get help.

'Stay right there, Mr Severin,' he said, 'I'll call an ambulance.' But he could not find the telephone.

He ran downstairs. There were no customers in the shop. William rushed next door to the Victualler's. The shop was also empty except for the butcher, Mr Flynn, who would surely know what to do. Flynn, presented with this unintelligible, babbling boy, rumbled: 'Hold on there, sonny. Calm down.'

The butcher came out from behind the meat counter, blood on his apron and sawdust in his hair. He was a fierce-looking creature with a ruddy face and hairy eyebrows. Big, butchering forearms. William was not a little intimidated by his very presence. Flynn shook William as the boy himself had tried to shake Mr Severin awake.

'Now, what is it?' Mr Flynn asked.

'It's Mr Severin,' William said. 'I think he's unconscionable.'

Flynn called the ambulance which came in half an hour and the gardaí, who took longer. Meanwhile, a small crowd of curious locals had gathered in the shop. There were more people here now than at any time when Mr Severin had been alive.

The ambulance arrived, all screaming sirens and flashing lights. Two young ambulance men dismounted and went in the back of the vehicle. They came out with a stretcher and pushed through the crowd, into the shop.

'Upstairs,' William said.

In a few minutes, they came back out, with Mr Severin on the stretcher.

'Nothing to see here, folks,' said one of them, imagining that he was an American television policeman. Starsky, perhaps.

'What is it?' asked a woman, anticipating the response as if Mr Severin had been her husband and she was in line for his life assurance money.

'Heart attack,' said the ambulance man, clearing a path through the crowd. 'Nothing we can do for him now.'

They put the stretcher into the ambulance, climbed in the front and drove off. The crowd began to drift apart.

William stayed put, along with the more prurient of the onlookers. A few minutes later, a couple of gardaí arrived in a white squad car. More sirens and lights. They got out to take statements and disperse the crowd which was already thinning in the wake of the ambulance's departure. Inside the shop, sitting down, William told the gardaí everything that he knew about what had happened. Work here. Upstairs. Severin. Dead. Shock. Butcher. Ambulance. Cops. I mean, yourselves.

The gardaí offered to drive him home, if he would just be a good boy and sit tight until they had finished checking the place out.

'I'll walk,' he said.

'Suit yourself, son,' one of the gardaí said.

William was free to go. He stepped out, closed the door of the shop behind him and skipped across the road to the window of the electrical store in which a display offered toasters, irons, hair dryers, LPs.

He felt in his pocket and found thirty-six pence and a conker. It occurred to him that he might never be able to afford the Casals boxed set, even if Mr Smythe had it in stock right now and was willing to trade it for thirty-seven pence and a conker.

The boy pushed open the door of the electrical store and went inside. It was a dark, musty place that smelled of old boxes and dust. All kinds of electrical goods hung on wall displays or hogged space on the counter behind which Mr Smythe was sitting, smoking a Woodbine and reading the *Times*, which he must have got from another newsagent. The man was either deaf or he had been oblivious to the commotion across the street, because he did not mention it. Maybe Mr Smythe was simply indifferent to the affairs of his neighbours, even when they were matters of life and death. William felt funny about the whole business. How was he going to explain to his mother why he had lasted only half a day in his new job?

He walked over to the LP rack, a small one between the trouser presses and the electric kettles. What wonderful titles, he thought. *Brain Salad Surgery, Tales From Topographic Oceans, A Trick Of The Tail.*

'Can I help you with anything?" Mr Smythe asked rather stiffly, peering out from behind his newspaper. But William was lost, fingering through the records, admiring the artwork and imagining the heavy melodies latent in the grooves, waiting for the needle to complete the circuit between artist and listener.

No Place Like Home

1. Late Summer 1997

How little they knew each other now and how long they
had known it. But, as Jordan Casey woke up in her old bed
one Tuesday, she felt that she and her mother had finally
begun to communicate. It was no longer strange to be
rising in her childhood bedroom. The clock on the bedside
locker said eight thirty-five.

Outside, the elm tree was dappled in the cold light of
another summer morning in Beauville. The leaves were
still fresh with night rains. Through her open bedroom
window, Jordan could hear cars go by on Emerald Street.

Her room was now very different. Where once there
had been posters of Duran Duran and Cindi Lauper on the
walls, covering accidental rips in the floral wallpaper, now
there were prints carried north from San Francisco over

previous summers. *The Atomic Alphabet* by Chris Burden. Italicised statements by Jenny Holzer. And Jordan's favourite, a detail from *Amour Reanimated By The Kiss Of Psyche*, mouths cropped in close-up.

In one corner, there were abandoned clothes across a wicker chair. A potted spider plant webbed out from another corner.

Jordan got up and had a shower. As she stood under the hot spray, she observed her body: breasts heavier than usual, she figured, though their size did tend to fluctuate; backside with the small traces of cellulite that she did not even want to think about; hair black, long and wet across her shoulders; belly bump not yet showing. She got out of the shower, took her time over drying, then she went back into the bedroom and pulled on a pair of jeans, a green shirt and flat blue shoes.

Her mother called from downstairs. 'Breakfast, honey.'

Jordan went down, thinking, as she did every day, of Jeremiah Alt, lost to her in San Francisco.

In the kitchen, she sat at the table, its polished maple top covered in a checked cotton cloth. There was a short stack of pancakes and a pot of coffee there, beside two plates. Her mother, Ellie, was dishing out some scrambled eggs. 'It's a beautiful day,' she said as the two women sat down together.

Jordan, 24, expecting. Ellie, 58, menopausal. Each of them had now survived a man. In Jordan's case, it was a boyfriend. In Ellie's, a husband. This had forged a new bond between mother and daughter.

'I keep thinking that the phone will ring and it'll be him,' Jordan said as she began eating a pancake.

Ellie knew not to say anything. Her husband, Dwight, Jordan's father, had died five years before, of a sudden allergic reaction to a peanut, in a Motel 6. Ellie had never heard of such a thing. A peanut killing a man.

At sixty four, Dwight had been about to retire from his job in the local library. He had been looking forward, she remembered, to long days walking the Labrador that had, as it happened, outlived him only by a couple of months. He had also been relishing the prospect of finally reading Harold Robbins all the way through, every bulging book from cover to cover. He had been a reader, that Dwight, a stalwart of the local Rotary Club and a fine dancer of the Twist.

When he had died, Ellie had found herself coping by imagining that he was still around. She would turn in bed at night and remember his strong arms warm around her waist, his nose brushing against the nape of her neck, his breath on her shoulders. It helped her to recall the tenderness of which Dwight had been capable when the occasion demanded. And she knew that Jordan would learn to cope with her own loss, eventually, although right now, that was small comfort.

Jordan was looking for a job, but, at her mother's urging, was not going out of her way. Jordan took her mother's advice. For her part, Ellie was glad to have her daughter back home from the city. She could do with the company. In return, Ellie intended to look after her for the duration.

'It'll be just fine,' she said, covering Jordan's left hand with her right. 'It'll be fine and dandy when things settle down.'

After breakfast, Jordan washed the crockery and cutlery. Ellie went out for the walk she was accustomed to, over to Harry Street, up to Williams Bridge and back around the town, before stopping off for the regular coffee morning at Carolyn Jones's house, down the road.

Jordan, too, went for a walk, but it was only as far as the small garden behind the house, which was an old mock-Dutch place passed down, it seemed, through Dwight's bloodline, though it was no more than seventy years old. As she stood under the old elm at the back wall, she looked up at the window of her bedroom and thought she saw Jeremiah there, leaning out, taking the air, ready for another day. The son of a bitch.

2. Spring 1997

Jordan had been working in the local Ahab's Café on Union Street for six months, having applied for the job because she liked the idea of an occupation that combined reading with coffee. It had turned out to be a perfect space in which to think about what she was going to do next. Back up north, the previous summer, she had come fifth in her third year political studies course at Albert University, though she had not stayed to complete her degree. Maybe she would eventually become a librarian like her father, but the idea of the lifestyle put her off.

She was sharing an apartment with her boyfriend, Jeremiah, on the northern fringes of the Haight. It was colourful, a boho flat filled from the wooden floors to the plaster ceilings with his taste. There was a poster for *Electric Ladyland*, framed in black metal, in the hall. Jordan did not like to see so many naked women on the wall. It made her feel violated; but Jeremiah had been in this apartment first and had made few concessions when she had moved in. It had remained his space.

3. Summer 1995

Jordan met Jeremiah during the summer of her second year in college. She had come south to San Francisco mostly to see the city but also to get a job that would help her save for next year. She found employment in a small art gallery on the Haight, near the Red Vic Theater. It was strictly small-time stuff, she soon discovered, no-one famous. Mostly, the artists were locals, acolytes of Rauschenberg, Rothko and Andy Wozniak, an outsider whose innocent faux-hippie collages were beginning to sell for five-figure sums. Valley girls with too much time on their hands and Silicon Valley boys dabbling in technological art: these were the clients that the Gallery represented. Jordan did not like much of the art that was displayed in the space, which was called Art's, after the owner. It was a name that only some people construed as having been mis-punctuated. Art considered it an in-joke between him and his friends.

Jeremiah walked in one Saturday, introducing himself as the artist whose work was currently on display. Then he took a stroll around the various exhibits. Later, she would find out that he was really a computer salesman with a sideline in art installations: the motherboard as city, the mouse as airship, the keyboard as Periodic Table.

'Look,' he said, as he ambled, admiring his own work, 'this one's called *Technopolis IV.* See: the metal parts are streets and buildings. The green areas are forests and public spaces. Come on, take a look.'

Jordan walked over to him. He was standing by a piece mounted on a stand. 'Here,' he said, 'kinda obvious, really, but I like don't recall it ever being done before.'

There was nobody else in the gallery except Art himself. He was in one of the back rooms unpacking crates of pictures. Jordan thought that Jeremiah was one of the most beautiful men she had ever seen. Up close, he reminded her of Ethan Hawke, the actor. Black shoulder-length hair, tidy goatee, a face that she imagined demonstrated Italian ancestry. She reached over to him, slipped her arms around his neck and kissed him square on the lips.

'Whoa!' he said, unused to such spontaneous admiration. She shushed him with another kiss. In the embrace that followed, Jordan and Jeremiah knocked over *Technopolis IV* and its stand, breaking the sculpture on the ground.

'It's only art,' Jeremiah said, on to a good thing. He continued to allow her to kiss him. Then, Art walked in.

'What the hell do you think you're doing, young lady?' A nasal whine of protest from her employer. He was a short, thin man in a black shirt under a black linen suit. Closely cropped grey hair. Spectacles with octagonal frames. His face was melting in sudden anger. She thought that it might drip and ruin his clothes.

Art combined his anger at Jordan with such profuse apologies to Jeremiah that the artist was beginning to get slightly embarrassed. He attempted to defend her. 'Really man, it's not her fault. Don't take it out on the babe, man.'

'You're fired,' Art said to Jordan. Jeremiah calmed him, accepting his apology and asking if any of the pieces had been sold, then engaging him in polite conversation. Jordan thought herself forgotten about, despite the fact that she was standing right beside Jeremiah, until Art boomed, 'You still here?'

She left. Jeremiah said, 'Later,' to Art and followed her out into the glorious, scorching Saturday.

They took a streetcar down to the Castro. It was Jeremiah's idea of freaking this country girl out. On the way, they traded names, dates, current life circumstances, star signs and blood groups. They stood behind the big handle in the middle of the vehicle that Jordan took to be the brake mechanism.

On a street, while looking in a shop window at some jewellery, they heard a man say sweetly, from behind them, 'Oh, why don't you just buy it for her!'

Walking past a street corner, after Jeremiah had understood that she was not, in fact, freaked out, they overheard a couple of guys: 'Let's buy some popsicles, go home and have sex.'

'Beer?' suggested Jordan, as they walked.

'You heard what the man said,' Jeremiah replied. 'What flavour popsicle would you like?'

She spent the last two weeks of that summer in San Francisco with Jeremiah. They went out a few times. He devised a program of entertainment for her: essential things to do when you've got only two weeks left in SF. During weekdays, however, he was unable to accompany her, due to his having to work all the hours of daylight in his office. He would see her nights and weekends.

Jordan found out a lot in those two weeks. He was a six-footer (she measured him with a tape one night while they were both drunk on Californian wine, standing him up against the jamb of his kitchen door as she might a growing child). His hair was naturally black, not out of a bottle. He liked Jimi Hendrix and Imperial Teen. He preferred Letterman to Leno.

His mother was a script doctor. His father, whom he never saw, except on videotape, was an actor on a daytime soap. He was an only child who had once wanted to be in a band, just to get laid. Not much to ask. He was the best damn computer salesman in the city. He fantasised about the potential of VR, cybersex and nanobots.

One night, they had rushed sex in his car, at a bizarre angle, on Nob Hill. The following Saturday, they stood at the top of Coit Tower, looking out from the nozzle at Alcatraz island, which was wreathed in mist.

'Do you know,' he said, 'Clint Eastwood is the only man ever to have escaped from the Rock?'

The next day they took the ferry out, chased by seagulls swooping down on the passengers who stood on the top deck, their cameras flicking like lightning-fast eyelids.

Ashore, inside that terrible place, they followed the tour, wearing the little yellow-and-black walkmans that provide the soundtrack.

'Over here is where Machine Gun Kelly got his.' Sound effect: knife squelching into flesh. 'Up there is the gallery where armed prison officers stood watch over the three levels of the main hall.'

It looked, to Jordan, like a battery farm for psychopaths and malcontents.

'On this level, just to the right, is the cell where Robert Stroud, known to some as the Bird Man of Alcatraz, spent most of his days except when he was working in the library.'

'My father had something in common with the Bird Man,' she said. In the museum bookstore, Jeremiah bought a heavy hardback copy of *Stroud's Digest On The Diseases Of Birds* and gave it to Jordan as a gift. Then they went out into the exercise yard and walked around. Jeremiah could imagine the frustration of being incarcerated in this place. The view of the bay and the city must have been an intense experience, he figured, if you knew that this was as close as you would ever get to it. Seeing cruise ships go by must have been a painful reminder of your status as an inmate. 'Boy, the Feds sure knew how to wreck a dude's buzz.'

Back on the mainland that evening, they walked down to North Beach and drank Scotch whisky until four in the morning in Vesuvio Café. From her seat, Jordan could see the green, triangular building where, a guide book had told her, Zoetrope Studios was based.

'We're tight,' she observed with glee at one point during the night, leading to a conversation about various terms for drunkenness.

The following Saturday, Jordan went back to the apartment off Union Square that she had been sharing for the summer. She collected her personal possessions and stuffed them in a holdall. Her roommate, Silvia Corso, a student from Turin, was out. Jordan left the apartment, took a streetcar north and walked the rest of the way to Jeremiah's place. Jokingly insisting that her dismissal from the job at the gallery had been his fault, he had, to all intents and purposes, been paying her way since. Now, she had some dollars and intended to take him to lunch. But when she arrived at his apartment, she saw a note on the door.

J, in Burnel's. x J.

Two blocks away, she found him in Burnel's, a little seafood place with a big menu. He had already ordered, sitting at the counter, his head in his hands. Today's special was Red Snapper. Two other customers sat nearby, arguing loudly about just how gorgeous Matt Le Blanc really was, on a scale of zero to kerjillions.

'What is it?' Jordan asked Jeremiah, putting down her holdall, getting up on a chrome-topped stool.

'You're leaving.'

'I'll phone,' she said, taking his right hand, placing it on her knee, then covering it with both of hers. 'I have my third year to do. Anyway, we can see each other between terms. You can come up to Beauville, if you like.'

'Can't leave my job,' he said. 'I'm the best damn computer salesman in the city.'

They ate lunch in silence. Jordan had clam chowder.

Tearful goodbyes at the bus station.

4. Summer 1996

Jeremiah took her driving around the Grand Canyon. It was said that it was not possible to stare into this abyss without experiencing the grandeur of nature, the insignificance of humanity and an intimation of eternity. Jordan said, 'Wow.'

'We stole this land from the Indians,' Jeremiah informed her as they stood on the edge of a precipice, all weathered oranges and impossible depths.

'Yes,' said Jordan, 'but where did we put it when we stole it? There seems to be some missing.'

By the time their trip was over, Jordan had decided to stay in San Francisco, get a job and move in with Jeremiah.

5. Summer 1997

Jordan had become well used to the customers. There were the sharp-suited businesswomen popping in for large paper cups of scalding Kenyan. There was the little African woman with her Bible. There were the tourists she would see only once, but would think of as regulars: Japanese with their cameras and eager smiles; Irish wanting to know your history, in case their ancestors had been related to yours; out-of-staters with their small-town big backsides. She would meet the occasional transient who was always the same person to her, no matter which body she saw him in: HIV-positives, paraplegic Vietnam vets, Gulf War syndrome sufferers, speculators destroyed by recession, people who had fallen between the cracks in life's sidewalk.

***

The day had begun like the one before and the one before that. Cold spring air. Petrol fumes. Steam rising from the grilles on the street. Greasy tincture of subway train peculiar to large cities.

She had taken over the float and the shift from Pilar, a Puerto Rican student who was studying political science, Jordan's old specialty. Two other colleagues were at various stages in their own shifts. Betty, a sophomore at

State University, taking Russian Literature. Sheridan, a local AIDS activist and helpline counsellor.

Outside, the street moved behind the window like a daily eight-hour film. Customers walked in off the screen into this little world with its green livery everywhere, its bookshelves full of Vikings, Farrars and Knopfs, its small, round, green tables and its paper cups of coffee.

At around ten, while Sheridan was busy in the stock room and Betty was over in a corner, collecting spent cups and wiping table tops, a man came in. He had a briefcase and seemed to be in a hurry. The pinstriped suit he was wearing was out of fashion. Jordan guessed that he was in his late twenties. Probably worked in something financial. He walked up to the counter, ordered a small Costa Rican coffee to go. As Jordan poured the coffee, the man put a dollar on the counter and picked up a book from the rack beside it: *The Bridges Of Madison County*.

'Your coffee, sir,' said Jordan. The man put the book on the counter.

'Thanks,' he said and took his coffee. She handed him his change, a quarter. 'Are you from Madison County?' he asked. He sounded like he came from around here, but so did everybody, no matter where they were from.

'Beauville,' Jordan replied.

'Uh, nice meeting you,' the man said.

'Have a nice...coffee.'

The man walked out. Just like that. Jordan followed his back until he had gone deep into the movie outside.

Another customer caught her looking at the man as he left. It was the African woman with the Bible, a regular patron. Jordan had not seen her come in and now felt embarrassed that the woman had observed her watching him.

The lady said, 'I'd like a large French roast. And one of those supersize chocolate-chip cookies. I know I shouldn't, but the Lord is hungry today.'

'Says nothing in the Bible about chocolate-chip cookies,' Jordan said, good-naturedly, 'last time I looked.'

'You leave the Bible alone,' the woman said.

'Sorry,' Jordan smiled, pouring the French roast into a paper cup. She reached into the counter display and with plastic tongs, removed a chocolate-chip cookie the size of a saucer. She placed it on a small paper plate, which it covered, and pushed it, with the coffee, towards the lady who shuffled with her Bible, finally putting it into her inside coat pocket. It was spring, but for some reason this lady needed to wear such a heavy coat. Black wool. Red neck scarf. The woman was wearing too much make up.

Jordan waited on her payment. 'That'll be two fifty-five,' she said.

The woman had to take the Bible out of her coat again to find her pocket book. She left the Bible on the counter, on top of the Waller book, fished out three dollars and handed them over.

'Things are getting worse,' the lady said. 'Three dollars for a coffee and a cookie.'

'I don't decide the prices around here,' Jordan said, taking the money, feeling bitchy. She went to the till, made the change and turned. The lady was already sitting down at a table, munching on the soft, honeyed cookie, worrying a chocolate-chip and turning the pages of Deuteronomy to find a favourite passage.

Jordan went over to her, put the receipt and the forty-five cents on the table. Betty was walking towards the trash can, having picked up a handful of paper cups and plastic spoons.

'You all right?' Betty asked.

'Fine,' Jordan said as she walked back behind the counter.

'You look a little pale, is all,' Betty said.

'I'll be fine,' Jordan said, embarrassed to appear unwell.

Betty took the black plastic liner from the trash can, brought it out back. As she passed Jordan, she said: 'Just asking, is all.'

Jordan saw the copy of *The Bridges Of Madison County* on the counter. She sighed as she lifted it, intending to replace it on the shelf. But on the counter, under the book, like an insect beneath a rock, was a business card. She picked it up.

Robert Sullevan. Architect. Telephone number, address, email.

Jordan slipped the card into the pocket of her uniform. She took the book by the spine between her thumb and forefinger, as though handling something distasteful, then she reached across the counter and replaced it on the shelf.

Robert Sullevan. Well, he didn't look like an architect to her. Unless he had his pencils in that briefcase. Unless he had drawn those stripes on his suit by himself.

For the rest of the day, she was too busy to think about him much. But she did allow herself a small daydream during her coffee break. She found it funny that those who worked in coffee shops should get coffee breaks. At eleven-thirty, Betty took over the counter for a while. Sheridan, a long, thin, handsome thirty-year-old, suddenly decided that he was not feeling well, and went home. Jordan sipped her coffee, a strong continental blend, by which was meant European rather than South American, and she thought about the architect. Anyone else would have given him no more than the uninterested glances she herself gave to other customers, with the exception of the Bible lady, whom she thought cute, despite her obvious insanity. But there was something about his walk, she thought. Maybe he was an architect after all. Or an artist, like Jeremiah, who hadn't had another gallery outing since the one at which they had met.

Her coffee break over, Jordan came out front again. An hour to lunch and already the street was getting busy with office traffic. Luckily, she thought, this place didn't do lunches, though it would have its share of rollerbladers, vee-pees, checkout operators. All human life, she thought, then poured herself another coffee, even though it was not allowed. Then, sipping on the quiet, like a teetotal alcoholic, she felt in her uniform's shirt pocket for the business card and the thought of going home tonight to Jeremiah began to annoy her.

At five-thirty, her shift ended. Jordan went out back and changed from her uniform to what she called her civilian clothes. A brown leather jacket, checked shirt, blue jeans, sneakers. She got her handbag from the safe and left. She walked a couple of blocks then took the BART home.

The front door of the building was open. She went in, climbed the stairs and took out her keys. Rattling them in the door, she listened for sounds inside. Jordan entered to find that Jeremiah was not there. He must have gone out for a walk.

Having taken off her jacket, she sat down in front of the television. *Roseanne*. Restlessly, Jordan flicked around the channels, couldn't focus on any of them, then got up and went into the kitchen with its small formica table. The drop leaves were up. Jordan began to clear the breakfast things. Beside the crumbling wholegrain loaf, bought from the Walgreen's across the street, she saw a scrap of paper, but thought nothing of it until she returned from the sink to continue clearing the table. This was no shopping list. She read, without taking the note from the table:

Jordan,
Fired today. They said I stole parts for my art. Best damn computer salesman in the city.

'I hate myself and I want to die.' – K. Cobain, saint.
I'll be in the Bay.
xx
Jeremiah Alt, loser.
P.S. Rent's paid for a month.

Jordan took the note, read it again. She did not say anything to the empty apartment. It did not occur to her that tomorrow was Independence Day.

***

The cops came, questioned her. A search off the coast brought up nothing, though an *In Utero* t-shirt and a pair of sneakers were found on the bridge. 'These look familiar to you?' After that, the police told her that there was no point in looking for his body. He was simply gone, like so many others.

***

Three days after his disappearance, she went to Golden Gate Park and spent the afternoon walking there until she had gathered the courage to go to the bridge itself. As you headed for Marin, the left-hand side was closed to pedestrians, though it was the right-hand side that people threw themselves off, facing the city, defying it.

She began the trek across the bridge, feeling it sway in the wind. It was tempting to just take off over the rail.

Looking up at the stately first tower that was still some distance away, she imagined what it must have been like all those decades ago, to have worked on this bridge, at the mercy of a gust or a slip. Had Jeremiah really taken the plunge?

Although she was not walking briskly, in twenty minutes or so, she made good progress. She could see tiny people ahead, joggers. Cars went by in both directions. In a city where smoking was regarded as all but obscene, it was curious to her that the automobile was allowed to thrive as though cars and not human beings were the dominant species.

Marin County ahead. Over in those hills, she reflected, must be Skywalker country. But she did not go that far. The walk had done her little good. *Damn Jeremiah*, she thought, *damn him, damn him, damn him.* She turned and walked back towards the city, furious with herself and with him. Out there, to the left, his ghost was now tramping the tourist route down the main hall in Alcatraz, like Machine Gun Kelly being stabbed in the back every day, eavesdropped on by a thousand pairs of uncomprehending ears.

***

Waking up alone the day after her walk across the bridge, she thought that Jeremiah was still there. His guitar. His *Electric Ladyland* poster. The ouija board that she would never let him use. His computer parts, waiting to be turned into sculpture. His t-shirts: *Nevermind, Rage Against The Machine, Axis: Bold As Love.*

She breakfasted alone on a bagel with ham and cream cheese. She drank dark Kenyan coffee, stronger than she usually took it. Today, she thought, I'll resign from Ahab's. I'll get a job at the box office in one of those multiplexes in Japantown.

But as she was leaving to go to work, she took ill and barely made it to the bathroom before she threw up. *Oh, Jesus*, she thought, *I shouldn't have had pig in that bagel.* She phoned in sick. Betty was distressed at having to cover for her.

Jordan called her mother. Then she spent the rest of the morning packing her bags, wandering around the apartment in a daze, unable to settle anywhere. She could do without most of the stuff here, but there were some items that she wanted to keep. In the afternoon, she telephoned a freight company, because she did not feel like carrying Jeremiah's things in her luggage.

Before the freight people arrived, she went out to Walgreen's and bought four pregnancy testing kits, just to be sure.

1. Late Summer 1997

Ellie was still out at her coffee morning when the van arrived at the front gate of the house. Jordan answered the door. The man had brought Jeremiah's belongings from San Francisco. She signed for one large parcel. Apologising unnecessarily for not helping the man to carry it ('I'm pregnant.'), Jordan stood in the living room as he brought it in, then she thanked him and saw him out.

It was nearly eleven-thirty. In an hour or so, the kids from the school would be out. Office workers would be facing into their last half hour before going to Wendy's or McDonald's or Spiteri's for lunch. Jordan reflected that she was no longer working in a service industry. She began to open the package with her hands, then stopped and got a carving knife from the kitchen. She slit the tape that bound the flaps on the top. All that remained to her of Jeremiah were the objects in this box. Vinyl records, stolen computer parts, a hash pipe, a couple of sculptures, a few t-shirts.

She had not taken everything but, before returning to Beauville, had called his mother in case Mrs Alt would like to have his guitar and amp, his stereo and speakers, his bong and ouija board. Through sudden tears, Mrs Alt had said she was grateful that her late son had been loved by such a considerate young woman. Jordan had not stayed for the Baptist memorial service. Nor had she mentioned her condition to Mrs Alt.

Now, Jordan went about the house and gathered a few keepsakes to add to this store of memories. She found Jeremiah's suicide note and put it in the box. Then she put in an unwashed pair of her panties, so that his ghost would remember her body; a copy of the *San Francisco Chronicle* that she had brought home with her; and a kiss, planted on the inside of the box, after she had smeared her lips with carmine lipstick.

Finally, she wrote a note on the back of a large postcard that had never been sent from San Francisco but had nonetheless arrived in Beauville. On the front, there was a picture of Alcatraz island, solitary in the Bay. The note, in her tiny handwriting, read:

Dear baby,

You will be 18 when you read this. I won't have told you that this box exists until then, so, surprise! These things belonged to your father, who was Jeremiah Alt, a San Francisco artist. He died, age twenty six, on July 3, 1997. It is now July 15. I hope that the world you're born into will be a better place by 2016. Your dad, I'm sure, would have loved you had he known you and would not have killed himself. You'll probably have heard everything from me by the time you read this. Just remember, no matter what ups and downs we have over the years, I love you. I hope we still like each other when you're 18. (You can tell me now.) And you've grown up right. Your loving mother to be. (I don't know your birthday or if you're a boy or a girl). xxxxxx, Jordan. PS. I hope this box hasn't decomposed!

Then she put the lid on the box and sealed it with brown tape that she got from a kitchen drawer.

Ellie arrived back half a minute later. Jordan heard the key turning, the door opening and closing, and her mother walking in the hall.

Ellie came into the living room, saw her daughter standing beside the re-sealed box. Jordan's lips were all red. There was a carving knife on the floor. She had a roll of tape in one hand.

'Are you all right?' her mother asked.

'Yes, mother,' Jordan replied quietly. 'Help me with this box.'

'What are you talking about?'

'Help me take it out into the garden.'

'What on earth are you doing with lipstick on your face like that?'

'Just help me.'

Ellie sighed. The two women bent down, as though the box contained dark matter that was too dense to be carried by mere humans. But Ellie found that it was not actually that heavy and she lifted it on her own.

'Where do you want it?' she asked, as Jordan stepped back.

'Outside.'

Ellie, lifting the box, followed her daughter out to the back garden. They stopped beside the elm tree.

'Will here do?' asked Jordan's mother.

'That's perfect,' said Jordan. 'Thanks. I'll do the rest.'

'What's wrong, daughter?'

'Just go back in the house and I'll see you in a while,' Jordan said. 'I haven't gone crazy,' she reassured Ellie, who frowned, but turned and went inside.

Jordan found the shovel in the coal bunker and began to dig a hole for the box. It was not difficult, because last night's rain had softened the soil and the sun was weak. She did not know how long she dug, but when she had finished, there was a trench into which she lowered the box. Then she buried the remnants of Jeremiah Alt in the earth of home.

'Are you done yet?' Ellie called from the back door, seeing Jordan put the shovel back in the bunker.

'Just about,' said Jordan. 'Is lunch ready? I'm starving.'

As she walked towards the house, she felt a sudden exhaustion. She put her hands in the back pockets of her jeans and stretched, yawning. In the right pocket, she found the business card that Robert Sullevan, Architect, had left on the counter in Ahab's. Jordan took the card out and looked at it. Then she tore it into little pieces and threw them to the wind like premature confetti.

Is It You, Sam?

Sam woke up in a front room of an apartment somewhere, not remembering how he had got there. It was a winter Sunday, probably about nine or ten in the morning. The first thing he noticed was that there was a young woman beside him. She was still asleep and she was not his wife, Rosa. They were both naked, under covers that seemed old-fashioned to him: animal-print throws, leopard and tigerskin patterns. His head hurt.

Sam stirred. His left arm was trapped under the neck of this lovely woman whose name he could not remember. Gingerly, he attempted to withdraw his hand. As he did so, she moaned in her sleep, moving her head. Taking advantage of this, he pulled his arm away, as one might whip a cloth off a table without disturbing the place settings.

The room was partitioned by closed French windows. On his side, there was a black leather suite that comprised a couch and two armchairs. A yucca tree stood erect in a Turkish vase. Otherwise, there seemed to be no furniture or features apart from the two naked people under these throws.

On the other side of the closed French windows was a kitchen. It was modern, constructed of steel and glass, with a hardwood floor. Terracotta pottery was racked on the worktop. The kitchen must have cost a fortune.

He could see his clothes on one of the black leather armchairs but for now, he contented himself with lying naked beside this woman whose name was returning to him. How embarrassing, he thought, if she woke and he could not recall who she was. Consoling himself with the possibility that she might not remember him either, he lifted one of the throws and regarded her body next to his. He found it easy on the eye and congratulated himself on his luck.

He decided to get up. Then, he thought that if he left the bedding before she woke, she might not take it too well. Especially if they'd had a good time last night. What a dilemma. He nudged her gently a few times but stopped when he heard a sound from the other side of the French windows. The door to the hall was opening.

Sam flopped into playing possum, under his cover, with one eye, barely open, on the kitchen. The man who came into the room was tall, broad-shouldered, hairless and totally naked. There was a large tattoo of a bald eagle on the man's back. A ring on each ear made him look like a pirate. For all his strangeness, the man was familiar. He walked into the kitchen then, and sat down on the floor, in the lotus position. Staring through the windows in the direction of Sam and the woman, he began to intone a mantra.

'Ommmmmmmmm.' It was a low sound, barely audible. Sam could not tell how long the man kept it up, but when it was over, the odd fellow began to do yoga exercises. Sam watched, fascinated. He had never done any yoga exercises.

Through all of this, the woman did not wake. It was only as the man was finishing up that Sam's sense of having seen him before crystallised into recognition. His name was Blank and he was a mime artist that Sam had seen occasionally in Washington Square Park, usually on Saturdays. Blank would pretend to be a statue, standing stock-still for hours, impervious to the attentions of passing kids, old women, anyone. When not immobile, he could walk around the park with such imperceptible movement that it would take him hours. You'd swear that he wasn't moving but you'd come out of a store half an hour after having seen him and he would have somehow travelled twenty yards. Sam was surprised to see him here, in an ordinary apartment, on an ordinary winter Sunday.

Blank completed his exercises and, apparently without having noticed the people in the front, walked out of the room, closing the door behind him.

Well, Sam thought, it takes all sorts.

The woman was coming to. Sam lay back on the ground, gently pulling the leopardskin throw around his throat. He pretended to be asleep and listened to her waking up.

She yawned, turned, snuggled up to him without, it seemed, being conscious of who he was. Her hot breath in his left ear provoked the memory of a name. Jean or Janet.

Jean or Janet opened her eyes. Sam did not see this. She groaned, realising that there was someone beside her. She thought that he was asleep so she shook him, less gently than he had disturbed her. He pretended to wake up.

'Mnnnnh?' he mumbled.

'Good morning, Alvin,' she said, wearily.

Alvin. Oh well, thought Sam. There are worse things to be called. Like intruder. At least she did not seem to be angry with him, but why would she?

'Good morning, Jean,' he guessed, rubbing his eyes.

'You remember my name. Good sign.'

'What time did we get to bed?' he asked, scanning her face for a mood.

'About six, I expect,' she said. Jean was well spoken. He liked the sound of her voice. That probably made two of them.

'Do you know where you are?' she asked.

'Uh…no,' he admitted.

'Upper East Side. We took a cab from the club, remember?'

114

'Was it romantic?' he asked, thinking what a lovely apartment she had.

'Hardly. You were out of your head in the back. Me and the Armenian in the front.'

'Armenian?'

'The driver.'

By now they were sitting next to each other.

'Babes in the wood,' she said, pulling her throw up around her neck.

'Sorry?' He had been distracted by a glimpse of her nakedness.

'Us.'

'Right. Better fill me in,' he said, ashamed.

She bent over to kiss him. He could not focus on her properly. She had a black bob and a small, kind face with an upturned nose. Sam did not resist her kiss, which turned out to be a barely perceptible brush of her lips against his cheek, like a low-flying air kiss.

'We'd better get dressed before people come downstairs,' Jean said.

'I think people have already been,' said Sam. Did she really not remember his name, or was Alvin the name he had given her last night? Safer to play along.

'Early bird catches the worm,' Jean said, then surprised him by dropping her tiger throw and standing naked on the carpet, stretching to her full height, arms almost disturbing the light-fitting.

'You look beautiful,' he said, as she relaxed and sat down on the couch.

'Thanks,' she said as she began to dress. Black lace underwear. Short silver skirt. Black silk blouse. Draped over the couch was her coat, a fake fox fur. He could see her shoes, silver with high heels, in a corner of the room. Had she thrown them away in abandon, or because her feet had hurt?

She pulled on her blouse and was buttoning it when Sam stood up. Unselfconscious, naked, he sat down beside her and gathered his clothes. White linen jacket, stripy t-shirt. He, too, had been dressed for the summer – even though the chill and the rain had been particularly harsh the previous evening. But he considered himself hardy.

His blue silk boxer shorts had gone missing so he put his trousers on without them.

'You're not bad-looking yourself,' Jean said as she watched him put on his clothes. 'In fact, I'd say you have movie-star potential.'

'You a casting agent?' he asked.

'I was paying you a compliment.'

They continued to dress.

'I'm a bit dehydrated,' Sam said.

'I'm sure there's water in the faucet.'

As soon as she had dressed, Jean stood up, pulled the French windows open and walked through.

'French windows indoors,' she observed.

116

'You have a flair for the unusual,' he said, awkwardly, slipping both feet into his new desert boots simultaneously, then bending to tie them.

'I do. But this isn't mine.'

'What?'

'I don't live here,' she said. 'This is not my place.'

'Oh shit,' Sam said and sank into the couch. 'Then whose place is it?'

'Blank. Mime artist, among other things.'

'Friend of yours?' Sam got up and followed her into the kitchen. As he sat on a stool beside the bar, Jean was on the other side, taking some ground coffee from an overhead cupboard.

'Blank doesn't have friends,' she said. 'Want some coffee? After last night's performance, you probably need it.'

'Was it…ah…good for you?'

'Could say that,' she said, beaming a smile at the perplexed man.

***

Sam was due in Cupertino's at ten-thirty and he was late. This place was the hangout of hairdressers and would-be literary types. If the writers got talking to the coiffeuses, they could exchange style tips.

He had just ended a month of abstinence from alcohol embarked upon after a near miss while driving drunk. His confidence shaken, he had almost sworn off driving. Tonight, a Saturday, he had taken the subway. He arrived in the lounge at around eleven. Allen was already there, sitting on a stool by one of the glass partitions that divided the room into three. Couples and groups of friends sat in the booths by the window looking out onto Canal. There was a low-level buzz of conversation in the air. Over by the bar, young women sat with gin-and-tonics. Discussing Nancy Friday or The Rules, Sam conjectured. One woman, sitting apart, did not seem to be with them. She appeared to be in her late twenties, and was a brunette, wearing black and silver clothes. An intense look of concentration on her face, she was talking with an older man who wore a sharp suit that was just a little too formal for this place. He was a big fellow, bald, serious-looking. Sam took him to be a former boxer or circus strongman.

Anticipating just when Sam would arrive, Allen had already got some beers. There were two bottles of Pete's on the ledge, beside Allen's cigarettes and lighter. Sam took off his white linen jacket, hung it on the stool back and sat down.

'How are you?' Allen asked.

Sam replied with a question. 'Were you in work?'

Although it was a Saturday, Allen had been in the office.

'Few hours,' Allen said.

'Anything nice?'

'Northeast Air. Press campaign for Monday.'

'I went shopping today. Bought a pair of shoes. Look.'

Sam pulled up the right leg of his jeans to show off his new desert boots.

'Very nice,' Allen said. 'How much?'

'Hundred sixty-five.'

Allen nodded.

Sam relaxed a little and took a sip of his drink.

Soon, they were talking ads. Sam asked what the campaign was selling.

'Leg room.'

They discussed the campaign. Sam was in the same business, but freelance. He wasn't so sure about some of the concepts, but didn't say that to Allen.

Noticing that their bottles were nearly empty, Sam looked around for a waitress.

'Hey, waitress!' he called. There was one several yards away. She frowned, but came over anyway. She was young, perhaps in her early twenties, and she wore the uniform of the bar staff here, a black, short-sleeved shirt, white apron and black trousers. The logo over her right breast said: Cupertinos.

'What can I get you gentlemen?' she asked.

'Two more of these,' said Sam, waving his bottle at her. 'When you're available.'

The waitress made an about turn towards the bar.

'Nice ass,' Sam said, watching her go.

'So, have you seen Frieda lately?' asked Allen.

'Yes sir, I have.'

'How is she?'

'As good as usual.'

'You were going for a drink with her last week.'

'Thursday.'

'How'd you guys get on?'

'Good. We talked.'

'You talked. Did you get your filthy little hands on her?'

'Yeah,' Sam admitted proudly.

'Bad boy,' Allen said, then gave a little laugh.

'And...' Sam started, but he was distracted by the waitress who had returned with a couple of bottles. She placed them on the ledge and took the empties.

Sam handed her a ten. 'Keep the change, baby,' he said.

She did not come near them again all night.

Allen raised his bottle and took a sip. 'So, are you going to leave Rosa, move in with Frieda, keep banging 'em both or what?'

'Told Frieda I'd call her,' said Sam, 'but I'm not going to. I'm in too deep already and I think Rosa's getting the idea that something's rotten in the State of Denmark.'

'Rosa wouldn't be exactly cheering you on if she knew,' Allen cautioned. 'Remember, people, let's be careful out there.'

'Yeah,' Sam said.

'I won't tell if you won't. Where is Rosa anyway?'

'She's at home. Migraine. The usual.'

Stephanie's coming in later,' said Allen. 'You'd better be nice because I think she's been feeling guilty on your behalf, know what I mean?'

'You reading anything?' Sam asked, absentmindedly staring at the woman by the bar.

'What, you mean like a book?' Allen asked.

Stephanie had been to a late movie. By the time she arrived in the bar, the two men had finished their third bottles. She walked in and spotted them. Stephanie was thirty, stylish, with short, cropped, bleached-white hair and a long white plastic coat. Sam thought she looked appropriately wintry and he suspected that, deep down, she did not actually like him.

'What can I get you?' Sam asked her.

'Same as you guys,' Stephanie said.

He got up and headed for the bar. Stephanie sat down on his seat.

Sam said: 'Keep it warm for me.'

'Hey!' Allen said. Then, to Stephanie: 'How was Al Pacino?'

Sam muscled in at the bar. Beside him was the woman he had seen when he came in. She was still talking to the older man in the sharp suit, but when Sam put his elbows down on the bar, attempting to get the attention of a bartender and avoiding eye contact with the waitress, the man got off his seat and, his back to Sam, headed for the men's room.

The woman still had that intense look he'd seen earlier. She seemed desperately worried about something. He regarded her, lustfully. Then a bartender, his head tilted, came over to him.

'Three Pete's Wicked.'

The bartender nodded and wheeled away.

The woman coughed. Sam looked at her and smiled wolfishly.

'See you in Cyrano's later,' she said in a put-on husky voice.

Caught by surprise, Sam nearly pissed his pants. He turned away from her and stared dead ahead, into the row of bottles suspended upside down behind the bar.

Her bald friend seemed to be taking a very long time in the men's room. Probably doing coke, Sam thought.

The drinks arrived. Sam handed over a ten and waited for his change. The woman coughed again. He looked sideways at her. The bartender brought his change. Sam pocketed the money and lifted the bottles. The bald man was coming back from the men's room. Sam saw that he was not sniffing or rubbing his nose, as expected, but he did have a stern look on his face. Perhaps he had just executed a major corporate takeover and was out tonight with his wife to impress her with the story. Or maybe Sam's first couple of guesses had been correct and the man really was a retired Palookaville slugger or a circus act.

'Thanks,' Allen said as Sam arrived back with the drinks.

'Thanks, Sam,' Stephanie said.

'Someone's got her eye on you,' Allen observed, smiling.

'If I were a free man…' Sam said.

'I thought you were,' Stephanie said. 'I have your seat, though.'

'I'll stand,' Sam said, nervous now. If he were to sit down he would be facing the bar.

They spent the next hour or so brainstorming the campaign. They tore the skins off beer mats so as to write down half-thought-out concepts. They got several more drinks.

Just before the bartenders began to close up, Sam looked around. He saw that the woman's companion was putting away his cell phone, having finished a call. The man bent over, slapped what appeared to be forty dollars on the counter, kissed the woman on the cheek and walked out. It amazed Sam how one couple could keep their seats at the bar all night. It did not occur to him that if you stay put, you don't lose your place.

Sam, Allen and Stephanie decided it was time to go but as they were finishing their drinks, Sam noticed that the woman was getting up to leave, pulling her fake fur over her shoulders. Sam's face went red. Stephanie and Allen were bemused. As the woman passed them on her way out, she paused to say, 'Cyrano's.'

Sam, dumbstruck, watched her go.

'Quick,' he said to the other two, 'let's get out of here.'

'Cyrano's?' Allen asked. 'Before she arrived, you were ready for your bed. Now it looks as though you're ready for hers.'

'See you outside.'

Sam got up, put on his jacket and gulped the last of his drink. He walked over to the door and practically jumped out into the rain that had begun, pounding drops onto the sidewalk. Sam did not have an umbrella and his white linen jacket was not equal to these conditions. Once outside, he stood in the shelter of the bar's canopy, watching the woman walk across the road to Cyrano's, where the doorman let her in.

In a moment, as he considered what to do, the others joined him.

'You all right?' Allen wondered, wrapping his arms about himself against the cold and the rain.

'Let's go for one,' Sam said. 'Come on.'

'They'll never let us in,' Allen said, but he knew that they would. 'Act natural.'

Crossing the street, they could see that the front door was closed. The neon sign flashed on and off in the rain. They walked up the three steps and pressed the bell. A thin, elegant Algerian opened the door. He was dressed immaculately in a white suit. Although none of them knew his name, they recognised him as the regular doorman.

'Good night,' Sam said.

The doorman said nothing, but showed them in, with a bare smile. The door policy here was sometimes relaxed, sometimes not, and you could never predict what it would be like on any given night.

They walked through the short hallway to the stairs that led to the basement. There did not seem to be many people inside. Sam saw two seats at the small bar, behind which two French women, deliciously got up in black chemises and red skirts, busied themselves pouring wine by the glass for various patrons, mostly middle-aged men. A Tom Petty song chugged from the speakers.

Sam allowed Allen and Stephanie to take the seats while he stood. 'House red?' he suggested.

'Sounds good to me,' Allen said.

Sitting, Stephanie took off her white plastic coat and got the attention of a hostess.

'House red and three glasses,' she ordered.

The hostess nodded and went to fetch a bottle from a rack under the counter.

'So, is she here?' Allen asked.

'Can't see her,' Sam admitted, casting his gaze around the dark, smoky club. On the walls, there were framed movie stills of José Ferrer, Gérard Depardieu and Steve Martin, all with big noses. A ledge ran the length of the club, about twenty-five feet. Down the back there were square tables covered in red crêpe. At the centre of each table, a squat white candle burned in a shallow red glass holder. If this place ever closed as a club, Sam thought, it could reopen as a photo lab.

'Missed your chance,' Allen said. Behind them, the hostess was uncorking a bottle of house red. She had already set three wine glasses on the counter in front of them.

'I think you should take it easy, Sam,' Stephanie said. 'You're drunk and you'll regret it in the morning. Where's Rosa?'

'At home,' Sam said, sheepishly. 'You're right. Let's just have some wine. Forget about it.'

'Sure?' Allen sounded concerned.

'Yeah. I'll regret it in the morning,' Sam said.

They watched as the hostess held the bottle up to the light, showing the label. Stephanie nodded. The hostess poured wine into all three glasses and set the bottle down.

'I'll get this,' Sam said, reaching for his wallet.

'You will not,' Allen said. 'We split it. I couldn't do another bottle.'

Stephanie nodded.

'Your funeral,' Sam said. Each of them put a ten on the counter. The hostess was quick to take the money to the till. They raised their glasses. Sam downed his in one go.

'Easy,' Stephanie said.

'Sorry,' Sam said, but he was no longer looking at them. At the front end of the club, near the stairs, he could see the door to the ladies' room opening. The woman he had been following now walked out, still wearing her fake fox fur coat. She did not stop, but as she passed Sam, she gave him a nod. Allen and Stephanie looked away, but Sam was smitten. He watched her walk towards a table at the back, then sit down at the far end of the club, beside the double doors that led to the kitchen. There was no-one else at her table. She was looking at Sam.

He refilled his glass and took it to the other end of the club, leaving his two friends to the conversation they had begun.

Sam approached the table at which the woman was sitting. 'Mind if I sit down?'

She did not. 'Be my guest. The name's Jean, by the way.'

'Alvin,' Sam said. He put his glass on the table and sat down.

'What kept you?' she asked.

***

Over coffee, as they sat beside each other at the breakfast bar, Jean told Sam a little of what had taken place the night before.

'You came over to me in Cyrano's. But first, remember Cupertino's? I was there with Blank…'

'And you took me here?'

'He's cool,' she reassured him. 'We were having a quiet evening when he was called away. He was boring me anyway and I wanted someone to notice me. It's lucky I saw you because you did notice me – a lot.'

By now, a hangover was settling in for the day, marking its territory inside Sam's head like a bad-smelling, horny dog with herpes and kidney failure, fouling a lamppost. 'Got any Tylenol?'

'Not my apartment,' Jean reminded him.

'Oh.'

'You said you'd stay the night with me on one condition.'

'Which was?'

'That I didn't tell your wife, Rosa, and that I didn't tell your friends who were at the bar and could see everything anyway. They said goodbye to us as we were leaving. You were charming.'

'That's two conditions.' Sam's face went white. He sipped his coffee. 'Blank. That his real name?'

'You can ask him yourself when he comes down,' Jean said.

'I will,' Sam said, then drained the rest of his coffee. He was already feeling guilty about Rosa. 'By the way,' he said, 'my name isn't Alvin, it's Sam.'

'You told me that last night,' Jean said.

At that moment, the door opened. Blank came in. 'How are our lovebirds this morning?' he asked in a low, hoarse voice.

'Fine,' Jean said. She got off her stool and met Blank in the middle of the kitchen. He was at least a foot taller than she was, his great bald head shining in the light from the kitchen window. Jean, on tiptoes, reached up, kissed his cheek, then stood to one side. 'This is Sam,' she said.

'I thought you were called Alvin,' Blank groaned, still standing. 'I hate liars.'

'What did you say?' Sam asked.

Jean stepped out of the way. In a split second, Blank lunged at Sam and caught his head with a ferocious blow that knocked him off his seat and onto the floor.

'What the fuck?' Sam cried out.

'I said, I hate liars,' Blank repeated.

Deadened by the impact of Blank's fist, Sam lay moaning and holding his head.

'Ready?' Jean asked Blank.

The big man lifted Sam off the ground. Then, cradling him as though he were a baby, Blank carried him out of the room and down the hall. There was an open door at the end. They went through.

Inside, this new room seemed airless. There were no windows. The only light was from the doorway and a television set which was showing static. Below the TV, a VCR counter flashed the time. There was a black leather sofa. Blank dumped Sam on it then held him down. The smaller man struggled but Blank landed another killer punch to his jaw.

Jean walked in, with a syringe in her right hand. She depressed the plunger a little so that a drop of liquid spurted out.

Sam hated needles. He could not think what he had done to offend these people.

Blank's right knee pressed down across Sam's calves and his hands pinned the other man's arms to the sofa. Jean knelt behind Sam so that he could not see what she was doing.

She produced a scalpel from behind her back and held it up to his face. A rush of bile in his gut threatened to make him throw up. Then, she cut the cloth of his shirt, exposing the skin of his arm.

'Careful with that,' Blank grunted.

Jean jabbed the needle into Sam's arm, without the formality of sterilising the site with ether. A few seconds later, Sam blacked out.

***

When he came to, he was not in the apartment. He was lying in an alley between two overflowing trash cans.

His head and stomach hurt. His jaw felt as though it was on fire. His clothes were torn. Sam looked like a hobo and felt like a louse. His wallet was missing but there was a twenty in his inside jacket pocket, along with some change and his address book. On the page that said: *My name and address*, he found out who he was and where he lived. His fake Rolex was gone. He did not know what time of day it was or even if it was still Sunday. People were passing by the space at the end of the alley. None noticed him.

The sun was high and a cold afternoon light filtered through darkening clouds. Gathering himself off the ground, Sam saw that his clothes were even filthier than at first he had thought. Under his jacket, they were ripped to shreds. He was still woozy. The details of the crazy dream he had just had were indistinct. He remembered a needle and not much else. Panicking, he thought he had been mugged. Some bastard had taken his memory. At least he knew his own name. And Rosa's. Shit. Rosa.

Sam walked to the end of the alley and on to the street. A sign told him that he was on Mulberry. He figured that, in his current state, no cab would take him, so he set out to find the subway. And as he walked, he passed a bum, who tried to give him money.

***

It was already evening when Sam arrived on the stoop of his building. He realised that he didn't have his keys. He swore. Then he pressed the doorbell. Rosa answered the intercom. She was crying.

'Is it you, Sam?'

Thank God, he thought. But she did not open the door.

'Rosa, it's me, Sam!'

An hour earlier, a bike courier had brought one white lily with a note from Frieda, accompanying a package addressed to Rosa. She had opened it as though defusing a parcel bomb.

Inside, she found a videocassette wrapped in the blue silk boxer shorts that she had bought for her husband a couple of weeks before.

When Sam had pressed the buzzer, Rosa had been watching the tape. On the screen, lit by the first rays of dawn crawling in from the street, she had seen a man and a woman in a room.

Close-up. The woman, rocking back and forth on top of the man.

Extreme close-up. The woman was going down.

Pull back. The man. Babyhoneygodohgod.

Like a gauze over this, was a French window in which Rosa could see the reflection of a bald man, naked behind the lens.

Long shot.

'Is it you, Sam?' Rosa sobbed now into the intercom. 'Is it you?'

The Wow Signal

One morning in autumn, Dr Graham James decided it was time to split the logs that he had brought from the forest with the half-track. The biological-research station had several open fireplaces in the living quarters, a converted old stately home onto which the Department had grafted a metal and concrete laboratory block.

After a breakfast of ham from the pre-spiced treated pig he had been rearing until recently and an egg from his own modified hen, James set out to find the axe. It was in the stock room in the basement. He thought it too small for the job in hand, but the chainsaw had broken the other day in the forest and the axe would have to do.

He walked out to the back of the house where he had been keeping the logs and set to work, using one flat stump as a chopping block.

For the rest of the morning, the reports of the axe biting into wood rang out like primitive gunfire. There were no other sounds apart from the humming of the generators and birdsong drifting in from the edge of the forest.

Although he had been alone here at the time of the outbreak, he had expected a relief crew to arrive within a couple of days. Instead, an email had come through from the Main Laboratory in Trinity College: the whole island was in a state of quarantine. He was to avoid contact with other humans: nobody could predict how widespread the infection would be amongst the general population but it was known that the virus was airborne and that the incubation period was only a few hours. He had taken the needle which, Trinity expected, would inoculate him at least until the next mutation of the organism.

Now, he wondered if the virus had indeed mutated into a form harmless to humans. He might never know. Despite several emails and attempts to radio them, he had heard nothing further from the Main Lab.

James was forty-five that day, although he had almost forgotten the date. It was a month since the outbreak. The air around here was clear; the counter in the laboratory kept him informed of the quality of the atmosphere: so far, so good. Even though he had taken the antidote, he was never sure of how safe he really was. James sliced into the wood, whistling a tune and thinking of the irony of his situation, as he often did. This life he was leading, this enforced rural existence, had once been the pastoral dream of jaded city-dwellers.

In his early teens, at the end of the seventies, he had heard of German couples who had come to Ireland, taking their caravans over on the ferry from France and driving to Connemara where, selecting a prime piece of land, they had set up home. Many of them had bought plots, built cottages, introduced strangeness to the locality. They had come here to begin new lives as candle-makers, carvers, farmers, having escaped the conurbations of the Ruhr Valley, reversed out of lives lived at the speed of the autobahn, eluded, they thought, the shadow of the mushroom cloud. They were welcome, no doubt, but would always be outsiders.

You might find a German couple sitting half-dressed in the garden, one summer morning, breakfasting at a wicker table on wheaten toast and orange juice, having just had a dip in the icy lake that none of the locals would swim in, though they'd fish it.

Some of them were into computers. Once, when James had been collecting for the Boy Scouts, he had turned up at the door of one such couple. Two Germans in their early thirties who had settled in the town, they took him in, gave him herbal tea and biscuits. The man, who was called Wolf, brought James into the sitting-room and showed him his pride and joy, a computer that he had built from a kit, put together with a soldering iron. It was connected by thick cable to a monitor that looked just like a white plastic television set. The image on the screen was black and white with pixels the size of headache tablets. 'You will soon be able to play ping-pong on this computer,' Wolf had told him. Meanwhile, Sandi, Wolf's companion – marriage being a bourgeois institution, they cohabited without vows – sat in a corner, in a white vest and bright blue shorts, smoking a joint and listening to a Queen song on the turntable.

To complete his logging, he had gone into the forest and used the chainsaw to cut down tall Sitka spruces. He had watched them falling, crashing against other trees, then slamming into the floor of the forest. The human race, he considered, was falling too, finally in greater numbers than the thousands of trees it had once cleared out of rainforests, probably unleashing the organism in the process.

While chopping down these trees, James had not needed to shout 'Timber!' because there was nobody to warn. He had simply stepped out of the way and let himself feel the thunder of each tree's collapse in the soles of his feet. Then he had stripped away the branches. Having brought back five logs with the half-track, he had then used the chainsaw to cut them into blocks that now stood in a pile in the yard, like a premonition of fire.

Counting the rings on one of them, he discovered that these trees had been here for over four centuries. Complete family lines, whole political systems, entire religions had all come and gone since their planting, but there was no marvelling at this fact: it had taken minutes to fell one tree, negating the comparison. One in the eye for nature.

Then, the chainsaw stopped in the middle of a log, its fuse packing in suddenly, dragging James with it on its last, stuttering bite into the wood, until he let go and dashed out of the way. The saw flipped sideways, almost hitting him, then died, coughing blue smoke, on the floor of the forest.

One in the eye for technology.

Today, as he began to chop the wood, he had no such thoughts. He was the only man in all this wilderness. An observer would see him raising his axe; the axe encountering some invisible breaking point in the arc above his head, sending the blade crashing down on the section of log on the stump; the wood splitting cleanly, two halves falling to either side as the edge of the axe bit into the stump; James picking up one half of the split wood, pulling the axe out, replacing the wood and swinging at it again. In this way, he had been quartering blocks all morning. But there was nobody there to see. There were only satellites collecting data that nobody would receive. Transmissions from the upper-orbit warning system, global weather patterns, air-infection vectors. Their controllers were no longer in command, widowing the orbiting machines.

By mid-morning, James had almost enough fuel to see him through winter. He would store it in the basement where he kept the axe and other supplies. The stock room was big enough, having once been a wine cellar. As he continued to work, he imagined the recriminations down there, could the wood speak to the axe or take the chainsaw to task.

He broke for a light lunch of a cube-tomato, bred to fit on supermarket shelves, and another patty of pre-spiced ham from the treated pig. For afters, he had a stoneless melon designed to grow to the size of a clementine.

That night, James sat in the living room of the stately home, watching an old, and favourite film. This room was where he spent most of his time between chores. During the daytime, he had a clear view of the forest from the window. At night, its familiarity was a comfort. James was no longer used to the sound of his own voice. But the voices in the movies that he played over and over were friendly, almost family. He allowed himself this luxury, despite the drain on power, reasoning that when the generators finally packed up, he would feel better about not having used them frugally.

Against one wall of the room, stood an ornate mahogany table on which rested three computer monitors, towers and keyboards, beside a radio receiver that James always kept on, attached to an answering machine that would record any transmission.

Above these, screwed into the wall, hung ten racks of disks containing music, films and educational software. If he wanted to, he could navigate the solar system, following the topography of Callisto like a prospector, weaving through the rings of Jupiter and Saturn, parachuting through the soupy clouds of Venus. The disks were as much relics of a bygone age now as the Jack B. Yeats and Hilda Roberts paintings hanging on the other walls.

It had been some time since his last film. Tonight's treat was *Silent Running*, his reward for the day's hard work. As Freeman Lowell tended his plants on the *Valley Forge*, James thought he heard a sound outside in the darkness. With the remote, he switched the audio off, then he listened. There it was again. His "wow" signal. It sounded like the barking of a dog.

He got up from his seat at the computer terminal and went over to the window. If there was a dog out there, it had likely been attracted to the light of the monitor, which spilled out, illuminating the yard. James could see no dog. Neither could he hear one, now.

He stood by the window for a few minutes, just looking. Soon, he was no longer thinking about the dog, but was listening to the forest. There were still birds, so why would there not be dogs?

Shaking his head, James walked back into the room and turned the light off. If he was going to meet the dog, then let it be in the morning. He sat down at the monitor and continued to watch the movie, though he kept the volume low. He heard no more of the dog that night.

The next morning, James stirred awake in the four-poster bed, coming to from a dream of his dead wife, Julie. There was a photograph of her on his bedside locker. She was thirty-five in this picture that he had taken years before on their holiday in Port El-Kantaoui. Like himself, Julie had been a virologist. They had lived a comfortable life together in Dalkey, in a large house that overlooked the sea. Julie had suffered a needle-stick injury while testing blood for HIV, and died years later of pneumonia. The procession of illnesses she endured through the tertiary stage had broken his spirit, though she had borne them with fortitude. James had nursed his wife through waves of attack by every opportunistic infection that came along, but by the end, he had ceased to love her. He had never told her this.

Soon after her death, he accepted this post at the biological research station. It became his sanctuary, on the edge of a Wicklow forest that had once been a National Park. Some days, his old feelings for her returned and he missed her terribly. He thought of her whenever he felt frightened by this new emptiness, this silent world. The memory of her strength somehow gave him courage.

He got out of bed. After a quick, cold shower, he took his time over shaving, noticing that the blade was rougher this morning: soon it would be completely blunt. Today, he would check the plants in the hydroponics department. He would take a look for that dog. But first, he breakfasted on the last of the ham from the treated pig. There was a limited supply of powdered coffee left in sealed canisters in the stock room. After he had eaten the ham, James cooked up a pot and sat in the galley, drinking a strong mug of the stuff. Its aroma resembled that of Arabica, but he knew it to be artificial. He thought of Julie, her dark hair spilling across her back, the first time she had taken it down for him; her intelligent eyes glinting, telling him that he was the one for her; the ironic sense of humour with which she had anticipated everything he said and, in a good-natured way, debunked his often muddled theories about life and love.

By noon, he had finished his chores, some of which he had deferred from the previous day. Last night's dishes had been washed and put away. Clothes had been hung on the line at the back of the house. He had taken the daily readings from the instruments in the lab: air pressure, humidity, viral count. He had made his observations on the experiments that were still running, though he was beginning to wonder at the point of all this activity. There were more tasks to be performed before his daily rounds were through.

At around twelve-thirty, James went looking for the dog. A walk would do him good, he decided. He packed two cube-tomatoes and some other fruit in a small rucksack, took the double-barrelled shotgun from the stock room and set off. James figured that the dog would have either slept in the forest and was still roaming around, or it had moved on. Perhaps, the thought occurred to him, he had imagined the sound of the animal. A reaction to loneliness. Before leaving, he checked the pen behind the house where the hen was still alive; if the dog had come as far as the station, it had not been hungry. In case it should return for the hen, he took the bird indoors and locked it in the bathroom.

As James walked, he wondered if the only people left alive were those who had been quick enough to be inoculated. He assumed that scientists and doctors had managed it, along with government ministers, police, clergy: those who considered themselves to be indispensable. But he also imagined chaos as society tore itself apart, services and utilities breaking down, lawlessness cracking open like an old wound on whose seam the bandages had grown hard and had split.

In the forest, he heard the chirping of birds and the crunch of his own feet on fallen leaves. His watch told him that he had been walking for half an hour. A little way ahead, in the heart of the forest, he saw some objects that appeared to be man-made. He walked on. When he reached the objects, he found that they were the makings of a picnic, abandoned now. An open thermos flask, its contents long evaporated, fungus growing in place of the liquid it had once contained; hardened triangular sandwiches furred over with growth, a few chocolate bars still sealed: these items lay at random on a cotton tablecloth. Someone had been in a hurry.

For a moment he forgot about his search for the dog and now he scanned the area for bodies. Had these picnickers been caught by the virus? He could see no corpses, but he knew that the people who had been here were now surely dead.

From where he stood, he could no longer see the station. It was time to give up but as he started back, he heard a barking sound from some distance behind him. Cautiously, he walked towards it, raising his shotgun. Though possibly immune to the virus, the dog could be infected with rabies or worse, and was almost certainly wild now.

The barking seemed to ricochet off the trees as James followed it. Where was the dog leading him? In a clearing about thirty yards beyond the abandoned picnic site, he came face-to-face with the creature, and felt a small thrill of fear.

The dog stood, staring up at this man. It was panting, its tail erect, wagging like a needle on some gauge. Its mouth hung open, and James could see no froth around the lips, the tongue lolling to the right. He tried to remember the names of breeds. This one was a boxer-plus, a modified strain. James reached into his rucksack for a longlife apple.

'Madra,' he said, bending down to offer the apple with his left hand as he clasped the shotgun with his right. 'An bhfuil ocras ort?'

Instead of coming closer, the dog ran off and James went after it, wearily, having put the apple back in the rucksack. Like a good dog, it was probably taking him to the bodies of those picnickers. He had heard of dogs so loyal that they would attend their masters' graves for weeks or even months until they themselves died of neglect. This dog looked the sort, a friendly animal guarding the remains of the people who had fed and nurtured it from a pup. There might be no threat: even if the dog turned on him, James could finish it with his shotgun.

The animal continued to run. James was soon sprinting to keep up, dodging the ancient trees. All he could hear now was the sound of his own breathing and the barking of the dog. The trees seemed to fly past him. Ahead, the dog kept going. James realised that he was seriously unfit.

They had been running for several minutes when James saw the dog disappear behind a dense stand of trees. The sun was hurling spears of light down through the forest canopy; James imagined himself impaled on one of these shafts. He paused, then walked carefully towards the trees where he had seen the dog go.

As he approached, the dog appeared again, suddenly. It sprang from its hind legs, jumped him. James let off a shotgun pellet that slammed the creature against a tree. Nervously, he stepped back. The dog bounced off the tree and fell to the forest floor with a series of yelps that subsided into whimpers. Then it was silent and dead.

James walked over to inspect the body. Bending down, poking the dog with his gun, he could see where the pellet had hit. Blood seeped from the body into the earth. Dead leaves were dyed black. As he stood up again, he heard another sound. Behind him came a low rumble like a growling orchestra tuning up.

James turned.

Two dozen dogs of different breeds were gathered in a motley pack, preparing to attack him. Rottweilers, boxers, Labradors, Alsatians, greyhounds, mongrels, modified spaniels. They had been guide dogs for the blind, guard dogs, thoroughbred racers. They had been domesticated pets, ornamental companions, working farm animals. Some had been sheepdogs, sheep-killers, bird dogs.

James froze, horrified, with one pellet left and no ammunition in his rucksack. He stepped back as the pack advanced slowly. He aimed his weapon at the dog in front, a slavering Doberman that now began to pound towards him. As James pulled the trigger, the stock slammed into his shoulder.

The pellet missed the Doberman and cracked into the bark of a tree. This was a signal for the other dogs to attack. With terrifying speed, they descended on him in a bloody, howling cascade of claws and teeth. It was over in a minute. After the attack, the dogs gathered once more into a pack and headed in the direction of the station.

James lay on the forest floor like a corpse desecrated before burial. He felt the life ebbing out of him, his ripped flesh, his broken bones, all the pain in the world concentrated into one failing body. The sky was falling away. It was peeling off the surface of the planet.

Epilogue

He sees the ground from above. His eyes are missing, but he sees the ground. There is someone walking through the forest towards his body.

It is his wife, Julie, free of all blemishes, beautiful and clear as the day on which they had first made love. She is walking to meet him as he leaves his mortal frame. She is kneeling now, urging him to get up and walk, raising her arms, yearning to embrace his remains.

Julie is whole again. Before she can touch him, dead leaves begin to blow, whipped up by a miniature tornado, swallowing her perfect body and his. And then she is gone, reclaimed by the earth, a modern Persephone. James cannot tell where the underworld begins.

In his final moment, James sees something else, something impossible. He sees the dogs, running wild through the empty rooms of the stately home in search of food. He hears the radio finally cracking into life with a voice from the past, giving him the latest casualty figures. Six billion dead. Earth is a graveyard. The voice is chattering and random, pulsing out its syllables and stops, pounding out erratic time, like the broken heartbeat of the forest.

A short time later, another voice comes through on the radio, with only the dogs to hear. It is not a human voice.

Wake

Monday. Frances lies now, in the clothes in which she died, over the blankets on the neatly made bed. The farmer is looking at her: her jeans are too tight because, embarrassed by her spreading waistline, she had refused to wear trousers big enough to accommodate it comfortably. Her sweater is woollen, ribbed and black, speckled with white flecks. What passes for fashion in this part of the world would not cut it in Paris or Milan. Her shoes are black trainers that, earlier, he had removed and placed on the bed beside her feet.

Feet, he had read somewhere, swell when a person dies. Frances's ankles have swollen and her overgrown toenails seem to look down on them through her polyester tights.

She has lain in this bed for two days. What else could he do but bring her here to their room? Her wish had always been to die in her own bed. At the time, 'burying' her here seemed to be the next best thing. The bed is her territory now. The headboard is her headstone. He has carved her name and dates there with a penknife.

He longs to climb in beside her and hold her, but he fears that she will not let him. Besides, her stench is overpowering: stronger than the scent of love. She exudes the smell of someone who has ceased forever to wash. He will have to stop sharing a room with her.

It is getting time for final things. Tomorrow he might take her from the bed and bathe her body.

Tuesday. The farmer wakes to find blood dried on his skin where the head of a splinter has entered his arm. The sun is up. Judging by the light, he guesses that he has slept until noon. Outside, the cows are in agony, their udders weeping.

Having made his prayer for Frances's soul and kissed the poppy bruise on her temple where his Land Rover had hit, he goes down the stairs. The bruise is duller now, a progress report on her continuing decomposition.

In the kitchen, he pulls on some clothes, then he shaves, using the mirror over the sink to watch himself. The mirror is greased with use, accumulated fingerprints and dust. There are two cracks in it. The mirror will remember him long after he has looked into it.

Ultimately, shaving is futile. Growth is never kept at bay for long. This time, he playfully cuts himself once on each side of his neck. It is a game of join-the-dots with life itself. If he nicks himself often enough, he might slit his throat in instalments.

The clock over the fireplace reads a quarter past twelve. Before he milks the cows, he makes breakfast. Eggs, when cracked, give up their potential and are forced into another universe. He watches the albumen and nucleus solidify on the pan and thinks of lost chickens. Sausages go brown, then black. Pudding crumbles. He hates pudding, but Frances had always loved it. Potato bread: he thinks of blight. When it is cooked, he puts the food on a plate and makes tea: thick and strong like tar. He takes her breakfast up to the room on a tray and leaves it on the locker by the bed. Should she accept it, he will know that she is coming back. By five he will have gone up there again to make sure. More than likely, the food will not have been eaten and he will take it downstairs to the bin. Already there are two breakfasts there: symbolic meals. Since her death he has not made her lunch or dinner. That would be crazy.

The cows are growing more impatient by the minute. At one o'clock, he goes with a pail to the byre. Udders are now unbearably female to the farmer, reminding him of Frances.

When he begins to milk the first cow, he presses his head against the body of the beast. Eyes closed, he pumps the frothing liquid onto the ground. At the last moment, he dispenses with the pail, knocking it aside with his elbow. The milk streams over pebbles and grit.

He gives up milking and spends the rest of the afternoon reading a four-day-old newspaper. Across the water, a sheep has been cloned.

Here, there is no television: Frances would not have it in the house. There is a radio but it has been broken for two years. The only artificial voice in this house since then has been that of Jim Reeves, the singer, whom Frances had idolised. She had only one of his records and used to play it over and over again. *Put your sweet lips...* She had never recovered from his death in a plane crash all those years before. Since then, she had cursed aeroplanes.

The farmer had flown in one once, a Fokker 50 to Heathrow. There had been a lot of turbulence and that had terrified him, but the sight of clouds below him was sufficiently breathtaking to confuse his fear with wonder. He had spent the duration of the flight gazing into the vision of heaven that obscured the face of the Earth. The clouds had seemed to hold suspended between them little islands of land and water.

At five, as usual, he checks her room. She has not eaten. He takes the tray down the stairs and accidentally spills the tea on himself. Had it been hot, he would have felt more than simple annoyance.

In the kitchen, he feeds the breakfast into the bin and then rubs a wet sponge on his shirt where the tea has stained it. Then it is time to wash his wife.

Back upstairs, her rigor mortis makes lifting the corpse difficult. She feels heavier than usual and her body is stiff. He does not believe himself to have the energy to lift her all the way downstairs, so he gets a rope, slips it around her back, ties it and pulls her to the ground, dragging the blankets after her. He hauls her down the stairs. Her head bangs on each step in a sickening percussion. Panting with exertion, he pulls her into the living room and sets her on the floor.

He finds undressing her awkward, because this carries more shame now that she is dead than at any time during their life together. He does it with the light through the window making play on her skin and her clothes.

After he has untied the rope, it is relatively easy to remove her woollen sweater but her brassiere proves difficult. He has never got the hang of them. This one is a tan contraption. Frances had always undone her bra in the dark, with expert fingers, but he had always fumbled, whenever he tried to open it. Given the simplicity of the eye-and-hook design, Frances was usually unimpressed that his mind could not instruct his fingers sufficiently well to do this. Now, he dares not risk the opprobrium of a dead woman, so he cuts the bra with a scissors, but the scissors catches in the material and slips, piercing her skin. Angered at his own carelessness, he decides to use his hands but fails. He takes up the scissors again, shears between the cups and cuts the straps out of their fastening-hoops.

Then he removes her jeans. He undoes the buttons, takes the scissors again and cuts. It seems to be the right thing to do. Her jeans lie under her, opened like the skin of an orange. He tears her nylon tights off with his hands but uses the scissors on her knickers. As he pulls these garments away, he finds himself crying: the tights had given her skin tone a touch of warmth.

He sees that the injection scar on her shoulder has gone brown. Her hysterectomy scar appears whiter than ever. Maybe it is his imagination, but her faint, fair moustache, fine and invisible from a distance, seems darker. It is said that hair and fingernails continue to grow for a few days after death, or else the rest of the body contracts, to give the appearance of growth. His wife makes a masculine corpse.

Now, she is dead but not properly buried. He sits down for a few minutes on the armchair where he had earlier read the newspaper and looks out through the window at the unfeeling sky. He composes himself and stands up, gathering the clothes that he has cut from her and putting them on the sofa.

Then he takes the wheelbarrow from the shed into the living room and lifts Frances into it. It is a hearse of sorts. Wheeling her out into the shed is not easy; her body threatens to fall out. Her right arm catches in the jamb of the living room door. Her bare right foot knocks against a small table in the hallway.

In the yard, he lifts her out of the wheelbarrow. He carries her into the shed and leaves her on the ground beside the old copper tub. He puts three kettles on and fills two plastic eight-gallon containers of cold water from the outside tap, keeping them by the side of the tub until needed. He refills the kettles as soon as he has poured out their contents. It takes half an hour for enough water to boil, by which time the first few gallons have cooled.

Meanwhile, Frances has had to wait in the shed, her eyes seeming to look through the large hole in the roof at the sun going down. Darkness creeps back across the world, but he wants sunlight to wash her as his hands do, caressing her body with a love that he had found difficult to express when she was alive, despite his obsession with her.

He has to make it quick. It will not do to have to wash her by the light of fluorescent lamps. He lifts her gingerly from the ground and puts her in as gently as he can. Apart from the strong lingering smell of death, there are other signs of decay. Her bruise is brown, like the spreading flecks on the skin of a rotting banana. Her skin is taut and pale. Her face is zombie-like with the dead stare that makes coroners draw down the eyelids of the deceased, so he closes her eyes behind a wall of skin, her sockets healing over at last after the lifelong wound of sight.

Then her head slips under the water, her legs thrusting into the air. The thought that he loves this woman who is now only a corpse, induces mild nausea. He feels his stomach protesting but he manages not to throw up by gulping back the bile that makes a pang of indigestion in his throat.

Now, his Frances is in the tub waiting to be washed while the last of the sun edges towards the horizon, as though reluctant to illuminate atrophy.

He first pours cold water in over her, then hot. The water rises to about two inches under the rim. Her privates are girded by a watermark; the water laps around them as though they are an island and her legs are gigantic palm trees.

The sun is departing rapidly. He hacks a square of soap from a big pink bar that he keeps in the shed alongside the green Swarfega and several opened tins of paint, their crusts hard from years of disuse, their lids beside them, screwdrivers and brushes trapped in the dried paint.

He starts on her swollen right foot, working up a lather on his hands and rubbing between her toes, then down across the ball and into the instep, moving onto the heel. Her ankle comes next; he takes his time with this, his favourite part of her body.

Then: her shin, her calf, her knee, her thigh. At the top of her right thigh, his hands tremble. How can he bear to touch her there now? It seems profane. But then, it had always been an intrusion. He avoids the problem by moving on to her left foot, and as he works down the leg, scrubbing as tenderly as he can, he thinks of nothing other than washing between her legs.

The skin has lost its suppleness. He is ashamed to find himself thinking that her body may as well be that of a turkey hanging in a butcher's window at Christmas, plucked and disembowelled.

Wednesday. He wakes up with his face on Frances's pudenda. This has probably saved him from drowning in her bath water – he had fallen asleep, face down, between her legs. He finishes washing her when he comes to. It takes a little while to become aware of himself, aware of the world, aware of the cold sunshine.

His hands still tremble near her privates, so he moves on to her torso, rubbing gently in a circular motion until he reaches her breasts. She can feel no sensation through them now but for half a second, he swears that in there is the ghost of a warm, beating heart.

He washes her neck as though throttling her. He lifts her head as if to kiss it. He can see in her dead face that his Frances will never be coming back to him, but he does not believe it. Not yet.

Later that day, he kills all the cows. Done with such speed, the slaughter appals him, but he does not give up until they are all extinguished. He has to use the shotgun on twelve of them, the humane killer on the others. The cows had belonged to Frances and he can no longer have them around. Now they lie lifeless in the byre. He would burn the byre but a conflagration of that magnitude might be too conspicuous.

As for the other animals here, two pigs and four chickens, he realises that he has been neglecting his duty. And as for the dog, Bran has been dead for a month already, of dog cancer. They had not decided on a replacement.

Walking back from the byre, he considers it strange that he has had no visitors. Paddy Boyle from Two Mile Road Farm, a man who had courted Frances thirty years before and who is now a confirmed bachelor with a fine bit of land, usually drops by for a chat and a pot of her thick, treacly tea after Sunday Mass, still sniffing after her. It seems that the farmer is being left alone with his wife, as though the whole of heaven knows his grief, understands his sorrow, respects his right to mourn in private.

Bran, his beloved sheepdog, is buried in a mound beside a tree in one of the fields. Tomorrow the farmer will dispose of his wife's body, and let the cows and pigs and chickens go to hell.

Thursday. Making love to Frances was always a fraught and strangely shameful process. The light had to be switched off or the curtains drawn. Words would be exchanged to the effect that if her father could see them now, he would not approve. That comment was as predictable as sundown and it could lead to much dissembling.

– Did you, you know…?

– Go to sleep.

The act would proceed in the following manner. In one corner of the room, she would take off her clothes while he, in another, would remove his. They would get into bed and fumble around, groping each other without passion until he was ready to mount her. It would be mercifully brief, the whole thing over in a few minutes. A quiet battle for control of the blankets was often the only form of nocturnal communication between them.

That is how it usually went. Now, it is different. This afternoon, he brings her on the wheelbarrow back into the living room and takes her up on to the large oak table. He kisses her on the mouth. Her lips have shrivelled and the sensation is not altogether pleasant. He kisses her on the bruise and once on each dead breast. He greases her pudenda with swarfega and mounts her. When he has come, successful at last, he lies on top of her for some time.

When he raises himself, he takes a wet sponge and washes between her legs. His seed is now inside a dead woman. Maybe she will give birth to a ghost that is half himself.

He covers her with a curtain taken from the window of the living room. Then he makes a pot of strong tea and soon he is sitting beside her, slurping the brew, watching over her.

He spends the rest of the day gathering turf, taking the Land Rover and a trailer to their bit of bog, miles away. He brings a flask of tea and some cheese and tomato sandwiches wrapped in aluminium foil. He turns on the radio in the cabin and listens to country music. He works for an hour, disassembling a rick of already saved turf and loading it on to the trailer. As he drives home, he can see the sun setting into the horizon that he knows he will never cross again. The uneaten sandwiches and the untouched flask of tea on the dash tell him that he is no longer hungry for that kind of food.

He parks the Land Rover in the yard and, by the light of a gas lamp, he unloads the turf. When he has done this, he builds a bed of breezeblocks in the shed. Then he goes to the tree under which Bran is buried and cuts three long branches from it. He hauls these home and, as he arrives in the front door of the house, he drops unconscious in the hallway, banging his head.

Friday. It is three in the morning when he wakes up. His throat is dry but he can not drink water. He rises, takes himself into the living room and lies down on the couch. At six, he manages to stir himself. The clock on the wall mocks him with wasted time. He glares back at it and promises to waste no more. He walks out to the shed with two of the branches and plants them a few inches apart in a couple of breezeblocks. Then he gets the hacksaw and cuts straight down the middle of each branch, making two Ys.

Back in the living room, he takes Frances off the table, discarding the curtain that covers her, and puts her into the wheelbarrow. He wheels her into the shed. There, with the hacksaw, he attempts to cut her head off.

His heart is sick, his stomach heavy, but he draws the saw back and forth, back and forth, its teeth snagging at first on the skin of the throat. Then: the flesh. The fibres protest but the saw soon hits bone. He continues to cut through to the marrow. I am making a cabinet, he thinks, for Frances's Jim Reeves record. Finally, he is through the bone entirely, with the sound of the saw screeching twice-murder, its steady rhythm the sound of a steel heart shuddering to a halt.

More flesh. The skin around her neck continues to snag. The saw continues to bite. Back and forth. When he reaches the other side, the saw refuses to cut it cleanly. The head hangs loosely off her body, skin like a garment whose weave is making the act of tailoring difficult. The body is defying him. The skin is holding. There is nothing for the saw to get hold of without slipping. So, he puts it down and finds the scythe.

Frances's head looks up at him through dead, closed eyes. Her stench commingles in the air with the iron tang of blood. It frightens him to think of what he himself will become.

He slips the scythe, a big, unwieldy thing, under the skin that still attaches Frances's head to her body. Then he stands over her head, which lolls back, almost touching the ground. With one tug, the scythe cuts through the skin and the head is free, rolling into the dirt – but with this upward motion, the tip of the scythe bites into his left thigh, drawing blood.

He muffles a groan of pain, unwilling to acknowledge the wound or stanch the flow that, in any case, is not intolerably deep and will clot. He feels sickened and elated simultaneously. He drops the scythe, puts the head on her stomach and goes into the yard. Taking an armful of turf, he runs back into the house to get the other branch from Bran's sacred tree, and brings the whole lot back into the shed. There are firelogs and matches there. He snaps the third branch into small sticks and builds a mound of them on the bed of breezeblocks around a couple of firelogs. He adds turf, lights this bundle and places Frances's head across the two Ys that he had made with the first two branches, bending them towards each other to support it. Then he sits on a bench, watching his wife's head cook as, outside the shed, dawn breaks.

He has not shaved in days, nor changed his clothes. He is covered in blood, like a butcher after a day's butchering. From time to time, he turns the head and throws some more turf on the fire.

While her flesh is cooking, he goes into the byre and looks at the dead cattle. It had been easy to herd them in here. At first, they must have thought that he was going to milk them but after he had guided each into a pen, they had seemed to suspect something. As the first beast had dropped down dead, the others had begun to be scared. By the time he had killed the third cow, the remaining beasts were moaning in protest, stamping the dust, crying out until his gunshots, echoing through the building, continued to reduce their bothersome noise. And then, out of bullets, he had taken the humane killer.

As he views their carcasses, he feels a sudden kinship. What is a husband, he thinks, but a domesticated animal dispensed with as soon as its sperm stops being useful. Oh, he is bitter, now, he realises. And sad, too late, for the lost cows, those beasts that had never hurt him in any way other than to remind him of Frances. Their voices had become her cries to him from beyond a grave in which he has not yet lain.

The farmer goes back to the fire and puts more turf on. The hole in the roof is acting as a chimney but still, it is smoky in here and the burning, decayed flesh infuses the air with an acrid taste. It takes a couple of hours for her head to cook well, brain sizzling in its brain pan. Her hair has burned off. Her face is oozing and shrunken. He fills the time pottering about, tending the fire, clearing his mind.

Twenty minutes before he takes her head off the fire, he puts on some potatoes and carrots to boil, in the kitchen. He makes a small saucepan of gravy and as he does so it occurs to him that he could have used the oven for her head, but he does not consider why he hadn't done so. Too late now. It is accomplished.

He sets the table where they had last made love. Then he brings her head into the living room, using heavy oven gloves. He puts it on a plate with the carrots and potatoes. He sits down to an early dinner.

Saturday. This morning, all he wants to do is leave her remains in peace, though he realises that he has her mind and soul in him now, they are a part of him until the day he dies, and beyond. He feels ill as he digs a grave for her, under Bran's tree. It takes until noon to do it. He does not eat lunch.

When he has finished digging the hole, he goes back for the headboard and pushes it into the earth at the head of the grave. Then he takes the wheelbarrow and brings her body, along with the remains of her head, to the field. He lowers her gently into the tomb and, before shovelling clay into the hole and closing her grave, tamping the earth down with the shovel, he prays that God will forgive him for loving his wife so very much.

For the next couple of hours, he scrubs the floor of the shed to remove the blood. He knocks down the bed of breezeblocks, throws away the charred wood, shovels the ashes into the tub. Then he goes into the house and waits for the sun to go down.

By candlelight, he has a bath. The wound in his thigh is hurting badly. It has begun to fester. He shaves his face and pats his cheeks with aftershave. The mirror with two cracks in it seems to say hello to him, twice.

Having dressed, he walks upstairs to the bedroom and puts Frances's things into the wardrobe. Without fear, he lies down on the bed. The absence of the headboard is a reminder of her passing.

The farmer puts these thoughts out of his mind. Then, with the spirit of his beloved wife inside him, he settles down for the best and deepest sleep he has ever enjoyed.

House Angel

Sunday night. I am perched on the head of the bed, looking down at myself, the man who is sleeping and dreaming of all the years of accepting everything that came his way. What a lucky man he'd been, without even realising it. Now he has nothing but the memory of Annie beside him. She has gone and taken with her nothing from their life together. And yet she has taken everything. He is living in this house, surrounded by the change in her effects. He sees the mirror that she had used for her make-up routine, the brush with which she had teased her hair, the empty bottles of perfume, their caps lost and her scents escaped around the house. No matter that he opens the windows wide, these tinctures of Annie refuse to leave, even the wallpaper is impregnated with all her musks and unguents. If he tears a corner off and places it on his tongue, perhaps he can be with her, or maybe he will only smell like her.

But that's just sentimental bullshit.

The angel dreams this, watching over his own unconscious form, a man who is talking in his sleep.

'I'm gone,' the man is saying. 'I'm gone…' as if he can no longer tell the difference between himself and Annie.

He will wake soon, the Angel knows.

Dawn penetrates the drawn curtains, equalising the light in the room with the supernatural luminescence emanating from the Angel that is still crouched like a white bird-of-prey on the head of the bed, wings gathered around its body like a cowl. When daylight becomes equal to the Angel's light, the Angel will be gone. It needs darkness, else it cannot shine. Candle power is its enemy. It is eradicated by daylight. Its name, this Angel's name, is Uriel, guardian of Eden.

In this house, Uriel is not guarding Paradise but is jealously protecting the man from all harm. Gathering at the corners of the room, the same as every night, demons lurk, kept at bay only by the dust. Dirt repels them. Human skin, shed, wards them off. A filthy house is a protected house.

When the man wakes, he will not believe in demons or Angels. He will not remember his own Angel, the one that has come from his body, his own sleeping body, like a wisp of breath expelled from his murky innards to take a look around before being inhaled back into the deepest alveoli of his lungs.

During the day, Uriel lives in the man's respiratory system – if it weren't for meditation and emphysema, it would have no sex life at all – and rises like steam at night, for Angels can take physical form but are not made of flesh.

Angel and man live here now without the woman and her guardian. The man is driving Uriel a little crazy. It is not that the Angel disapproves of the man's newfound tendency towards tidiness and order. On the contrary, it bears this burden with heavenly good grace and only a little grumbling. It is not ours to choose the humans we must inhabit.

The man is called Simon. This name is dear to The Boss. But Uriel does not care for it. And complicating matters is the small fact that Uriel is Simon. Nothing is impossible for The Boss, and this, the merging of Angel and human, is The Boss's little joke. In guarding the man, the Angel has to guard itself. That way, reckons The Boss, the Angel will do a better job. And Uriel is dedicated, in its own way. It intends to convert Simon back to the ways of slobbery and sloth, just to be on the safe side. There is security in filth.

Uriel is dying for a smoke.

The previous Friday. Uriel had not got on particularly well with Annie's Angel, Michael, which was always blowing its trumpet, opening gates as though the wind were howling, even on calm nights, and acting like a bouncer on the door of the house when people came to call. 'The human can come in but no way you're getting in here looking like that, my son,' Michael was known to say to the Angels who would accompany visitors.

So, last night, Uriel sent Annie away by suggesting to her that Simon was having an affair. While Michael was out banging the garden gate, Uriel produced long strands of blonde hair from thin air and left them tangled in the sheets on their bed. Annie's hair is short and black.

When she found the blonde strands in the bed, she did not need her nurse's built-in lie-detector to guess that, as far as their marriage was concerned, it was game over. *My husband*, Annie thought, *has been nailing some floozy while I've been struggling with dying old men on the ward*. She held the hairs up, demanding, 'What the hell is this? And don't tell me you were eating angel-hair pasta in bed. Or really thin blonde pasta. Or were you eating a really thin blonde?'

As a husband, Simon was history. He protested his innocence. Annie packed her bags, threatened him with a stealthy injection of animal anaesthetic from the laboratory of her friend, the vet, and packed herself off to her mother's house.

Men are boils, thought Annie as she departed, *and this one's just been lanced.*

Result!, thought Uriel.

That Saturday (and some of Sunday). Now Uriel could take care of Simon without any interference. Now it could watch the place revert to its natural state: dishes unwashed in the sink, dust gathering on the mantelpiece, filthy floors, stinking toilet bowl, toothpaste squeezed from the centre of the tube. Small pleasures like this made life worth living. Uriel even looked forward to cigarette ash on the carpet.

But, distraught at Annie's departure, bereft, discombobulated, Simon took a turn. He cleaned the entire house from top to bottom. Uriel could not stop him, for it is powerless in the daylight.

Simon took the Dyson and vacuumed all the carpets.

He used up two whole cans of Mr Sheen and five boxes of J-Cloths on the woodwork, the fireplace, the windowsill, and the shelves.

He rearranged all the books in the bookcases in alphabetical order. He took the vinyl records out of their box and sorted them by artist, chronologically, starting with Anthrax and ending with Zavaroni, stacking them neatly in the storage rack under the Pioneer stack-system.

He bought some storage boxes from the stationery store in the local shopping centre and gathered all the papers and household detritus lying about the place, emptying drawers, filling the boxes with paid bills, till receipts, used betting slips, lottery tickets, photographs of Annie, his birth certificate, their marriage licence, his expired passport, his old driver's licence, a little book of proverbs to do with beer, a big book of condolences that he had stolen from a funeral, a badge identifying him as a delegate at a marketing conference, a lapel pin marking him as a Jedi Knight. All packed away.

The night after Simon had done this, Sunday, Uriel manifested itself gradually at the head of the bed. It was furious. It could scent the cleanliness of the room. The washed sheets. The clean curtains. The air-freshener. It could even smell the horrifying loganberry stench of the toilet duck in the smallest room. It knew that the records were all in order, that all the spines of the books on the shelves were straight and correct. Douglas Adams, Richard Bach, Carlos Castaneda…Sidney Sheldon, Craig Thomas, Leon Uris…

When Simon went to bed that night, Uriel decided to teach him a lesson. Just as Angels are expelled with the first breath of sleep, so they are reclaimed by the lungs with the first inhalation of waking. Uriel spent the night entering and exiting Simon's body at random so that, in the small hours, a hacking cough would wake him and as soon as he had returned to sleep, he would dream of being suffocated. In this way, Simon's second night without Annie made him miss her even more than he did already.

When dawn came and Uriel had entered his lungs for the day, Simon decided that he would call Annie and ask her back.

Later, at work in the marketing division of the multinational weapons conglomerate where he was a product manager, Simon stole a telephone call from the company and rang the hospital.

The following Friday night. Almost a week later, Simon and Annie faced each other across a rough-hewn wooden table at Pasta Mañana, a 'Mexitalian' bar and eatery. The whole place was hopping with Friday revellers, out after work, still in their office clothes. There was faux-mariachi music on the speakers. The bar staff were almost indistinguishable from the clientele, in their formal attire and attitude.

'It isn't so much the affair,' Annie was saying, 'as the other things.'

'But baby,' Simon protested, 'there was no affair. I don't know how the hell that hair got there.'

'Don't give me excuses,' Annie said, evenly, inwardly furious but outwardly calm, taking a big gulp of her gin-and-slimline-tonic. 'I've heard them all before.'

'You have? But I thought I was the only...'

'It wasn't me who put the used condom under the bed. I don't know where that letter came from. Who? No, it couldn't have been her you saw me with. She's dead.'

'Please,' Simon begged. 'It could have come from anywhere. On the train, I could have picked it up on my clothes from another passenger.'

'As long as that's all you picked up.'

'Annie. I want you back! There's no other way of saying it. I can't sleep, I'm moody and irritable, I can't eat.'

'No change there, then, apart from the eating and sleeping,' Annie said.

Simon felt in his heart that he had lost her. He sipped his Carlsberg. 'I mean, if there's anything I can do to prove to you that I didn't have an affair…'

'Forget it. I don't even know why I agreed to see you.' Annie began to get up, but thought better of it and sat down again. 'You always used to squeeze the toothpaste in the middle of the tube. Now, I'm not saying that's a capital crime. But pissing on the toilet seat and not mopping up after yourself, that's treason. Belching in public, how ever quietly, in front of me. And in company. Picking your nose then biting your fingernails. Eating finger food with a fork and fork food with your fingers. Letting off farts without a four-minute warning. Reading *Playboy* for the articles. Hawking loudly. Leering at women in the street, with me present. Listening to Queen after I've gone to bed. Stealing all the bedclothes. Running your fingers through my hair when you want your back stroked. Coming first then falling asleep. Not coming and then falling asleep.'

'You don't have to be subtle, you know. You can come out and say it.' But Simon was shocked to find out so much about her dislikes. He thought they'd done a fairly comprehensive list before they moved in. Now, they were attracting the attention of other patrons. Annie did not care. She had the bit between her teeth.

'…getting head but not giving it. Giving it but being tired. Sticking nudie women magnets on the fridge door. Keeping cooked meat beside uncooked meat. Leaving the lid off the mouthwash…'

'So we're back to the bathroom again.'

'We're back to the bathroom again. Letting empty toilet-paper rolls lie around. Dropping your clothes all over the floor for me to pick up. Leaving the immersion heater on all hours. Getting the shower water all over the floor. Do you want another drink?'

'I'll get it,' Simon said wearily. He motioned to a waiter who came over and took their order.

'I think I'd had just about enough of your habits and if you want me back, you'd better change your ways, mister, or I'm not damn well coming back. There's a queue of men out there, all waiting to fuck me.'

'All right,' Simon said.

'All right what?'

'All right, I'll change my ways.'

The following Sunday night. Uriel is looking sheepish tonight. Michael, as usual, appears smug as a boneheaded bouncer. They have agreed to disagree on the subject of whose style should dominate the household. It's an uneasy truce.

They are perched side by side at the head of the bed, eyeing each other suspiciously. Uriel is troubled by Michael's assertion that demons are not kept away by dirt, that it is the presence of the Angels that does it.

In the corners of the room, demons are muttering in anticipation of the Angels' letting their guard down. They're smoking their heads off, drinking rotgut whiskey, playing strip-poker. Once in a while, a demon will wave at the Angels. 'Hiya fellas. Wanna smoke?'

And every so often, Uriel tries to give Michael a dig in the ribs but Michael's wings get in the way. Below them, Annie and Simon are sleeping, entwined like a couple of newlyweds. Annie is smiling and snoring at the same time. Simon is babbling something unintelligible.

Amazed at how unfilthy the house was when she finally agreed to come back to Simon, disconcerted that he has stopped being wasteful, alarmed that he has not mentioned his ex-girlfriend since, Annie is nonetheless delighted to have him back. She had never believed in the hair anyway. She has started smoking, though, with her medical training she does not approve of the habit. When she lit up earlier, Uriel had inhaled Michael's secondhand smoke, wishing that Annie would change her brand to something a little more pungent than Silk Cut Ultra. It's like smoking fresh air, for God's sake.

Another day is coming on. Dawn penetrates the drawn curtains, equalising the light in the room with the supernatural luminescence emanating from the Angels. They are still crouched like white birds-of-prey on the head of the bed, wings gathered around their bodies like cowls. When daylight becomes equal to the Angels' light, the Angels will be gone.

Return Of The Empress

It was a Turkish Delight from La Maison du Chocolat that gave Clora Lynne the idea. She would become immortalised in her own special way. Certainly, she had been an icon of the small screen in Britain, in the 1980s, but her star had faded. Nobody now remembered that she had once ruled the vast, totalitarian Human Empire that had radiated from Earth as far as seventy light years. They remembered her frocks, yes, and her high heels; her long, flowing red hair and her outrageous make-up. They vaguely remembered the character, Leonora, but not remotely did they remember the actor.

As far as Clora Lynne was concerned, she had been the most glamorous thing in that BBC TV show, *Raven's Rebels*. Her antagonist, the bitter anti-hero, Raven, or, as the actor was called, Davison Ross, was another matter. He was still a minor celebrity and seemed these days to make a living on the convention circuit in the States. She had read on the internet recently that he had just done a commercial for haemorrhoid ointment.

Clora Lynne was above all that. She was beyond infinity, as it were. She could not bear to expose the aged whale that she had become to those young men for whom, thirty years earlier, she had been a masturbatory fantasy. Now, secluded in a luxurious Paris suite paid for by her divorce, Clora Lynne had turned her back on the world. Every one of her sixty years had gathered now, in the folds of her flesh hanging loose around her hips, in the deflated barrage balloons that had once been the most famous breasts in England, in the varicose tracery that seemed to hold her legs together, in the the old, sagging skin that was more like a carrier bag for her body, tied up in her hair that, though still red and long, had streaks of grey in it. Someone, she thought, someone should tear that bag open and perhaps, just perhaps, they would find a gift inside it.

In her youth, she had appeared in a number of Hammer films, usually as a virgin deflowered by a witchfinder, or as sacrificial jailbait, or as a bride of Dracula. Christopher Lee had once asked her out on a date, but she had turned him down on the grounds that he was, being immortal, too old for her. A spell on ITV's police drama, *Blue Light*, had taken care of the rent for a while, but in those days, television actors were paid hardly anything and besides, she had been much more interested in religion, so she had walked. One of those utopian Seventies cults had claimed her for a few months – spent in a spartan commune on an island off Scotland. Though uplifted at first, she soon tired of the Exegesis therapy and discovered that the politics of the place were far from utopian. They were, in fact, enough to drive anyone insane, so insane was what she went. When she returned to the real world she accepted a sudden marriage proposal from the American film producer, Ed Wallace, eighteen years her senior, and rich off the back of a few successful disaster movies.

Then came *Raven's Rebels*, in 1979. Suggestions in the press of an affair with Davison Ross had almost endangered her marriage to Wallace, but he had let the rumours pass, without ever quite believing her protestations of innocence. The truth was that Ross had, on several occasions, propositioned her. He had persistently begged to fuck her, in character. Every time, Clora Lynne turned him down. After all, Ross was himself married, to the steadfast and ordinary Johanna Fitch, a make-up artist he had met in the 1960s, while he was in rep in Leeds and she was nightly transforming him, a white man from Somerset, into Othello.

As the show became a hit in the UK, with over ten million viewers tuning in regularly, Clora Lynne found herself in the public eye. She did not like the attention but whenever there was a camera or a reporter handy, she encouraged it. She also did not like the conditions in which she had to work. There was not much of a budget on that show, so for all her high heels and camp frocks, the production looked cheap. Quarries doubled as alien worlds. Nuclear power stations were spaceports. The flats that formed the walls of her flagship used to wobble. The increasingly less salubrious guest artistes – at first the usual RSC types, and in later years, high-profile stars of light entertainment who could not act, but would draw in jaded viewers as the ratings took a nosedive – began to give the show a patina of tinsel which she found depressing. Five years into the show, Ross was the bigger star. After a particularly gruesome evening out with the cast, at the end of which Ross put his hand on her ass and asked her to join him in the green room for a hand shandy, Clora Lynne refused him one last time then threw a glass of Blue Nun in his face.

A week later, Ross had her fired. The producers informed her that at the end of the current run, she would be let go.

At least, Clora Lynne had thought, they'll have to give me a spectacular exit. A dramatic death scene. Instead, they simply wrote her out. She did not even appear in the last couple of episodes of the fifth series. Early in the sixth, a minor character alluded to her arrest and imprisonment in a coup. Leonora was replaced with a younger vamp, played by Candace Wells, a redhead who had once slept with Ross while they were both in a production of *Run For Your Wife!* in Scarborough.

However, at the end of the sixth series, *Raven's Rebels* itself was cancelled. The public missed me, Clora Lynne often thought to herself. That show was dead without me. I was Leonora, Empress of the Human Worlds, Lord Protector of the True Philosophy, High Admiral of all the Fleets and Successor to the Glorious Founder. And they wrote me out.

Three weeks after the show went off air, a tabloid story involving herself, a young fan and twenty gallons of drinking chocolate, ended her career, her marriage and her life in England.

These days, Clora Lynne knew, such a scandal would have meant that she would get her own chat show, a column in The *Independent On Sunday* and a recording contract. Despite everything, Wallace had been generous. He had just produced a series of Hollywood space operas and had negotiated for himself a large cut of the merchandise. Her divorce settlement paid for the luxury suite on the Rue du Faubourg St-Honoré. It paid the staff to be courteous but not officious. It paid for chocolate, which she still liked, as befitted an Empress, to bathe in. She had the men downstairs blend gallons of drinking chocolate for her and bring it up in the elevator, in drums. They would pour the creamy liquid into the bath, then withdraw discreetly. They thought her mad, or at least eccentric, but this was Paris. You could do what you liked, if you had money. She never had visitors. She rarely went out. The telephone almost never rang. Twice, early on, the night porter, Lamargue, had tried to interest her in a gigolo, but she had declined and nobody had suggested such a thing again.

Instead, she read Proust, over and over, for eighteen years. 'It seems to me,' she once told the concierge, Ribaud, before she was confident enough to use French, 'that if you are going to go the whole hog with Proust, you might as well do him the honour of taking as long to read it as he took to write it.' It did not register with Ribaud that she was being amusing. Neither did he guess that although she spoke with Received Pronunciation, she was actually from Carmarthen.

Alone, with a freshly delivered bath of drinking chocolate waiting for her, Clora Lynne would take off her clothes and stand naked in the hotel room. Appraising her old flesh in the mirror, she imagined herself being eaten out by a succession of fanboys, all of whom had, in their own tiny minds, jerked off to the sound of her evil laughter, each of whom had, in her daydream, to stuff her mouth with delicacies from La Maison du Chocolat, before she could come. Though standing, Clora Lynne would almost pass out with that fantasy of those little turd-burglars making love to her as she was now, rather than as they preferred her to be, before she would snap out of it and go to the bath and take care of herself. There, she would lie down, sinking in like a hippo, masturbating herself to a raucous orgasm. Often, she would gush. She would close her eyes as though succumbing to the deep, warm, anaesthetic of a chocolate death by drowning. It was the ending she had not been given, the ending she desired, the ending – on more than one occasion of falling asleep briefly before her breath geysered out – that she very nearly had.

Twenty years of this. People had given up on her. The boy, the young fanboy, had grown up and was now running a website in honour of the show and the woman whose career he had destroyed. He once wrote on his site that Ross had put him up to it. Ross's lawyers had made him take that posting down, though they had not closed the site. That boy, Clora Lynne knew, was in love with the fictional character she had played, and vilified the real her as a fake for having not lived up to his ideal of the Empress. She sometimes read his site at the computer in her master bedroom and wondered what would happen if they actually met again. She might have to strangle the little scumbag. Scandal was something that Clora Lynne was less comfortable with than fame. How had it been? In her chocolate bath, she would reminisce.

Terrence Elliotte had seduced her. His little fanwank fantasy was to be caught naked with his Empress. And he had succeeded. Oh, he had known how to get under her skin. They had met at a fan convention in Chicago, the last one she had ever attended. Elliotte – stupid name, she thought, for a stupid little fuckwit – had flown over from London to meet her. He had come up to her at a signing and got her to autograph the black-and-white ten-by-eight publicity photograph that showed her staring off into space, her hands around her throat. Appealing to her sense of vanity, he had bought her drinks that night at the convention's disco. He had bought her cigarettes. He had bought her expensive chocolates from a local boutique.

Elliotte had claimed to be nineteen and she had believed him. With sweet words she rarely heard in those days, he enticed her to bring him up to her hotel room. What he hadn't told her, and what she discovered suddenly as she lay naked in a bath of chocolate, expecting him to join her, was that he had also brought along a photographer from one of the London redtops.

The man burst in. Eight snaps later and she was finished. Her chocolate-covered breasts were all over *The Sun* a day later, accompanied by an interview with the boy who was now "in hiding for fear of reprisals by rabid fans." Even his worried parents did not know where he was, and the newspaper was not telling. On her return to England, reporters ambushed her at Arrivals in Heathrow. Back in her Kensington flat, there was a fax from L.A. It was Wallace, expressing disappointment in her poor taste and demanding a divorce. The police called around but took the incident no further than a few questions. Quite literally, in England now, she could not get arrested.

Chocolate was the only means by which Clora Lynne could have an orgasm. It had started in her teens when she found that, on eating a Fry's Turkish Delight while masturbating, the intensity of her orgasms was magnified. If she had her mouth stuffed with this chocolate, she would gush like Niagara inverted. Soon, she could not come without it. Eventually, she had taken to bathing in drinking chocolate. At her divorce proceedings, Ed Wallace cited her chocolate addiction as grounds. She found that, at least, quite amusing. He also cited the incident in Chicago. And besides all of the above, there were the enormous cleaning bills.

A luxury hotel suite in Paris, even one as deliriously well appointed as this one, with its three bedrooms, two lounges and ostentatious bathroom, all done in the style of Louis Quatorze, even a hotel suite in Paris with nine television sets, can be your very own Bastille.

Clora Lynne liked to watch television. Sometimes she would have a couple of sets in each room. Then, once in a while, she liked to watch all nine sets simultaneously, bringing them into the main bedroom, plugging them into a pair of extension cords, basking in cathode rays as though sunbathing in the light of fame.

When not taking chocolate baths, while chain-smoking Marlboro Lights, while cursing the terrible fortune that had brought her to this place and the enormous fortune that kept her here, she would revel in the horrors of European television. The French channels, with their subtitled crime capers, bad variety programmes and inept soap operas – made her think that, if she still had a career, she could have landed a lead role in any one of them. The Italian channels, with their porn-inflected news programmes, made her jealous of those slut housewives who were nobody until they exposed their breasts, whereas she had been nobody after she had done the same. On the German stations, all she could watch without laughing was *Raumschiff Enterprise: Das Nächste Jahrhundert.* It heartened her to see Patrick Stewart dubbed into very stiff German, as though a car salesman had taken over his voice. If only, Clora Lynne thought, if only I had auditioned for that show. I would have walked away with the part of Deanna Troi, who also liked chocolate. Given her then status as *persona non grata*, she had not received the call. It had occurred to her that, having had one role in a hit space opera, she was considered too famous. She had been too good for *Star Trek.*

In her heart, she would have given anything to have that kind of exposure again. She would even have accepted the role of Beverly Crusher. Her own show never appeared on German television. In truth, Clora Lynne would not be able to watch the beautiful young woman she had been. The icon. The Empress. Still, they could have sent her a DVD, though she had not even been asked to do a commentary.

Now, as she rose, she felt for the first time odd that she had left all nine sets on with the sound down, flickering silently through the night. She could not sleep without being bathed in the cold glow of television, and she always left them on, but now, this morning, it was strange to her.

In the shower, she found a lump in her left breast. She spent the rest of the day sitting naked on her bed, almost catatonic, watching the blitzkrieg in Iraq, the bathycolpian Italian housewives, the worst of French variety.

The following day, Clora Lynne decided to go out. It was a cold, crisp Wednesday morning in April, nearly eleven, when she rose from her bed where she had fallen asleep at some hour she could not remember. She did not order breakfast. She did not have a shower. Feeling her breast, she found the lump still there.

She went straight for the wardrobe and put on an elaborate black dress that had a starburst insignia on the front, and a high collar at the back. It was one that she used to be able to fit into easily but now it accentuated the flab around her belly and her legs. Black shoes that pinched her feet, a pearl necklace that Wallace had given her, and a black Prada handbag, completed her ensemble. She had not put on knickers or a bra. In the bathroom mirror, she looked like an echo of someone powerful. A deranged image of a glamour queen, she thought. Well, maybe that's what I am. The dress was the one she had worn in Episode 48, in which Raven had nearly succeeded in blowing her up.

Downstairs in the lobby, she went over to the reception desk. There was only Ribaud on duty, and no bell boy, and a few residents coming and going. A sour-looking couple in what she took to be their twenties, stood in front of the desk, checking in.

'Monsieur,' Clora Lynne said, regardless, trying to get Ribaud's attention. He was a wiry man whose skin looked like he had stolen it from a chicken. In his seventies, uniformed, circumspect, he seemed to Clora Lynne to be every inch the indifferent Parisian. In fact, he was from a small village near Antibes.

'Un moment,' said Ribaud.

'Monsieur!'

Ribaud ignored her. He smiled at the young couple, waiting as the man signed in. Then, Ribaud handed the key to the young woman. He did not call for anyone to help them with their bags so they picked up their own luggage and dragged themselves over to the elevator.

By now, Clora Lynne had taken a pad of hotel stationery, written something on it with a hotel pen, and torn the page off. She held it up for him. Ribaud turned to her. 'Madame Lynne. Je vois qu'aujourd'hui vous êtes l'Empress.' Impatiently, Clora Lynne gave him the piece of paper with her instructions on it. 'Je veux que vous obteniez ces articles pour moi. Chargez-les à ma pièce.'

'Certainement, Madame.' He took the paper, glanced at it and looked up at her with a wry smile at her stiff French.

As imperiously as she could manage, Clora Lynne turned on her heel and walked away towards the revolving front door.

Out on Rue du Faubourg St-Honoré, she headed for La Maison du Chocolat. As she walked, she observed the people: poor, stinking humanity. If Raven were here, with his powerful starship, *Emancipator*, he could have taken them all out with the push of a button. But he probably wouldn't. Even an anti-hero as bitter as he, had nonetheless been the good guy. Taking people out at the push of a button had been her job, until The Powers That Be had written her out.

Half way to the store, she stopped in the street to feel her left breast and although she could not detect the lump, she knew it was there. Perhaps, when she got to the shop, she could ask them to wrap it in hard chocolate and isolate it from the rest of her body.

La Maison du Chocolat was busy. They knew her there, but did not make that too obvious.

Every so often, Clora Lynne would turn up and buy a Boîte Maison, an artillery of intense bursts of pleasure, a variety of ganaches infused with the flavours of summer: apricot and lavender, melon and port, passion fruit and coriander. As she stood in the boutique, casting an avaricious eye over the displays, she tried to not notice other customers. They were in the way and this was her private paradise.

Today, she ordered something simple. She spotted five Turkish Delights, covered in dark chocolate, and immediately knew that she had to have them: one for every year she had been Empress.

Minutes after leaving La Maison du Chocolat, Clora Lynne was sitting outdoors at a small table, with a café latte and a glass of water in front of her. The waiter was, of course, rude, but the coffee was deliriously good. To her,

French coffee was the best in the world. As she sipped, she deliberated on whether to have the chocolates all at once or to save them for later. One orgasm for each Turkish Delight. That was the plan.

She put down her coffee cup and decided. Reaching into her bag, she took out the tiny box and put it on the table. Then she opened it, picked up one of the chocolates, bit a corner off, and came, there in the street, quietly, without anyone noticing.

It took her minutes to regain her focus and when she did, she found herself staring at the chocolate, a brown square with a little corner of pink where she had bitten it.

In that moment, something changed in her. She knew now what she would do.

Later that day, as she lay in her room watching television, Ribaud telephoned and told her that the items she had ordered were ready. He sounded sad on the room's old, bakelite telephone. 'I also have the number you wanted,' he said, in English.

Clora Lynne wrote it down. Then she got up off the bed and went to her computer where she emailed Terrence Elliotte to tell him what a little prick he was and that now she wanted payback for what he had done to her.

Davison Ross was at home when she called him that evening.

'What are you wearing?' he asked, after their awkward reintroduction and a few false apologies.

'Nothing,' Clora Lynne said.

'My God, woman,' Ross said. 'Have you no shame?'

'You know I don't.'

There was a pause. Ross broke the silence. 'Clora, listen. Why are you calling me?'

'I wanted,' she said, 'I wanted to offer you something.'

'Why now, when all those years ago I couldn't even if I paid you?'

'I'm dying, Davison. I have cancer. I want...to see what it's like.'

'I should think you'd hate me, after all the things I did to you.'

'You want to fuck the Empress,' Clora Lynne said. 'I want to fuck Raven. Bring your costume.'

'What's that you said?' asked Davison, suddenly registering an important fact.

'I want to fuck you in character.'

'No, about the cancer.'

'I have it. I don't know how long I'll have it, though. Cancer is like that.'

'I'm...I'm sorry to hear that. Listen, I've got to go to Milton Keynes tomorrow to do a Q&A with the fan club. After that, I'm in Birmingham to shoot a training video.'

'Do you want to fuck me or not?'

'Well, you're old now.'

'So are you.'

'I suppose...I suppose in character it would be all right.'

'How's Johanna?'

'She's fine. Fine. And the cats are fine, too. She's out with the girls tonight. Bridge.'

'Will you come?'

'That depends on what you do to me, you dirty wench.'

'I hate you, Davison Ross. But I want this.'

'Old girl,' Ross said. 'You were the only one who ever refused me. How could I resist, even if you are a fat old trout?'

'I'll fly you over. You can't be making much money from asshole cream.'

'You heard about that? Well, it beats being on *EastEnders*.'

Five evenings later, they sat having dinner in a dark little restaurant near La Bastille, Les Mouches. It was a cosy place, busy, with a couple of waiters dashing to and fro in a more or less comical, if random, dance. The walls were amber stone, broken by windows of etched glass. The furniture was bentwood and roughly elegant. At the back was a long zinc bar where Parisians sat and drank wine or coffee. There was, thankfully as far as Clora Lynne was concerned, no music.

They had already had their starters and now, Davison Ross tucked into a steak tartare while Clora Lynne picked at her veal chop. They were drinking a particularly fine Michel Lynch. The two actors seemed from a distance to be chatting amiably like old lovers.

Ross had left his bags in Clora Lynne's hotel room before they'd gone out for the evening. He was wearing a dark suit, with a white shirt open at the neck, like an orchestra leader gone AWOL. Clora Lynne wore a pair of black trousers and a blue silk blouse. She had washed.

Ross was well-preserved for his sixty-four years. No longer the dashing young man that Clora Lynne remembered, but his face was still handsome, and his body, while overweight, still spoke of someone powerful and well-fed. He had the appearance of a man who lived the good life. His accent, like hers, was RP, and seductive. No hint of his original Somerset remained. Perhaps he was putting it on.

After half an hour of reminiscing about actors they both knew, and dodging any real conversation, Ross said, 'I can't believe I'm sitting here in a Paris restaurant with you.'

'That,' Clora Lynne said, picking up a piece of veal on her fork, 'is because you never believe anything.' She swallowed the veal.

'A lady of your years should not be living in seclusion like this.'

'It's my choice now,' Clora Lynne said. 'At first, though, it was my only choice.'

'Well,' Ross said. 'We all make mistakes.'

She glared at him. He regarded her coolly.

'Remember Martin?' Ross asked, taking a sip from his wine.

'How's he doing?'

'He's playing King Lear at the Almeida.'

'Bastard,' Clora Lynne said.

'On our show, he couldn't string two words together.'

'He was a drunk,' she said, 'a liar and a wanker.'

'And a tart,' Ross said, 'though I suppose we all were.'

'Only, you, Davison. You'd jump on anything. Male, female, dissenter.'

'It's not my fault if I had a short attention span.'

'How's your meat?'

'Raw.'

'Unlike your performance in *Mother Goose*. Overcooked, apparently.'

'You didn't see that, surely.'

'I read about it on the web.'

'From that little shit who destroyed you?' Ross's face went white.

Clora Lynne paused and looked him in the eye. 'That was you, wasn't it?'

'I swear, Clora, on my mother's false teeth –'

'Nobody would ever dare to be your mother.' Clora Lynne picked up her wine glass and emptied it.

'I suppose you're right.'

'Anyway, that stuff is all in the past. I'm dying and it makes no difference.'

'I'm really sorry to hear that,' Ross said. 'But tell me one thing. You never wanted me. You never did. You threw a glass of *Liebfraumilch* over me.'

'It was Blue Nun. And of course I wanted you, but not like that. I didn't want to give in to your filthy little dick-brain.'

'Oh, Clora,' Ross said. 'If only you had said yes. I would have left Johanna there and then. You and I –'

'Don't be an asshole, Davison. I want you now, and that's enough.'

Two hours later, after a walk through the streets of Paris, during which they got increasingly romantic and sentimental, Clora Lynne and Davison Ross arrived back at her hotel. In her suite, they closed the door, turned on the lights and went into the master bedroom.

Clora Lynne had had champagne brought up. It was waiting for them in a bucket on the dresser, beside two flutes. There was a note from Ribaud which said, *Bonne Chance, Mme Lynne.*

'Open that,' Clora Lynne said. 'I'm going to the bathroom.'

Ross looked at the champagne and smiled. 'Don't be long,' he said. 'I'm horny.'

In the bathroom, everything was as she wanted it. The staff had filled the bath with chocolate. This time, it was not drinking chocolate, but thick, viscous, with the consistency of treacle. She pulled her knickers down, sat on the toilet and urinated, then got up, flushed, stepped out of her knickers and went to the sink where she splashed water on her face. Just as she returned to the bedroom, Ross popped the champagne and poured two glasses.

He handed one to her. 'To Leonora,' he said. 'Empress of the Human Worlds, Lord Protector of the True Philosophy, High Admiral of all the Fleets and Successor to the Glorious Founder.'

As he spoke, a startled smile spread on Clora Lynne's face. 'You remembered!' she beamed at him. 'That's who I am!'

And Davison Ross indulged her with a smile. They clinked glasses, then drained them.

'Let's get into character,' he said.

Clora Lynne put down her champagne glass and took off her blouse. She had been wearing no bra.

'My God,' Ross said, 'but you are old.'

'So are you, ass-cream man,' Clora Lynne said. 'Now let's not spoil things.' Then she took down her skirt and stepped out of it.

Davison Ross stared at her in wonder. He put down his own glass, went over to kiss her, but she backed away. 'Go into the other room. Your bag's there. Come back in here as Raven.'

'I brought the little leather costume from season four,' he said. 'You like that one.'

Clora Lynne smiled. Ross went into the other room.

When he came back, she had changed into her black starburst dress with the collar. Ross was wearing his Raven costume. His jaw dropped. 'You're...beautiful,' he said. 'Leonora.'

'Raven,' Clora Lynne said, channelling Leonora. 'I have you in my power and nothing in the world can save you now.'

They met in the middle of the floor and threw themselves into an awkward embrace. On the show, when they kissed, the rules were that their mouths never really connected. Now, there were no rules.

'Your friends are dead,' Clora Lynne said, after she broke away from their kiss, 'and your secret base is even now being overrun by my stormtroopers.'

'I…' Ross said.

'That's where you're wrong,' she prompted him.

'That's where you're wrong,' Ross said. 'Even now, the *Emancipator* is in orbit, ready to pluck me from this place. I'll not be your prisoner for long. But first…' he gripped her jaw in his right hand and threw her to the floor. She fell back, in an ecstasy of defeat.

'But first,' Ross continued, 'I have to kill you.'

'You'll never do it!' Clora Lynne hissed, from the floor. 'My guards will burst through that door any second now!'

Ross got on his knees and pounced between her legs. He took her starburst dress and tore the skirt, ripping it open. She grabbed his hair and buried his head in her pussy as though rubbing a dog's nose in its own mess. Then she pushed him away and said, 'Not yet.'

Ross backed off and knelt before her. 'What do you mean, not yet?'

'I mean,' Clora Lynne shouted, picking herself up off the floor, 'that you are not worthy to ravish the Empress of the Human Worlds!'

Ross stood up. 'Oh well,' he said. 'I have to go to the bathroom.' And he went.

Clora Lynne, in the torn dress of Empress Leonora, sat on the bed, waiting for him. She expected him to cry out in surprise, but he did not. Instead, he went about his business then returned as though nothing was unusual.

Calmly, he said, 'I see the bath is full of chocolate.'

Clora Lynne nodded and got up.

'Well if that's the way you want it, Leonora,' Ross said, gruffly, 'then I'm going to have to cover you in Arcturian Love Paint before I fuck your brains out, Your Majesty.'

Excitedly, Clora Lynne rushed to him and made to slap his face. As expected, he grabbed her wrist and once more threw her down, this time on the bed. He set to work, ripping the rest of the dress off her. In the wreckage of her Empress's gown, Clora Lynne gave in to him.

Ross lifted her up, not without difficulty, as neither of them was young, and carried her into the bathroom. All the way, Clora was swooning with delight. 'Raven,' she mouthed. 'You have defeated me. My armies are yours. I...surrender.'

In the bathroom, as gently as he could manage, Davison Ross lowered Clora Lynne into the bath of chocolate. Then he took off his clothes as if to join her.

204

'No,' Clora Lynne said. 'I want you naked, in the bedroom. Wait there for me.'

So, bemused, he did.

For a few glorious moments, Clora Lynne wallowed in chocolate, thick as a mud bath, not watered down as she usually had it. This time, she would be caked in the stuff, absolutely brown. She did not make herself come. When she was done luxuriating, she got out of the bath and did not towel herself off. Covered in the gloopy substance, she went into the bedroom.

Stunned, Davison Ross watched as Clora Lynne lay down on the bed and raised her legs as though giving birth. She opened wide for him.

'I want you to lick me,' Clora Lynne said. 'Gently, just my pussy.'

And down he went.

When it was over, when Clora Lynne had gushed, and when Davison Ross had licked her pussy clean, she pushed his head away. 'Look at me,' she said. 'Stand up and look at me.'

Ross did as he was told.

'You see the pink bit?' Clora Lynne asked him. 'You see the pink bit in the middle, between my legs? And the rest of me covered in chocolate?'

Ross nodded.

'I'm Turkish Delight,' Clora Lynne said.

Ross threw back his head, laughed like a maniac, and jumped on her again.

They made love five times that night. That is to say, Ross came once, prematurely, but his penis was not exactly the little trouper that, in his youth, had made entire chorus lines trip over themselves to get to him. Clora Lynne came five times. Once, when Ross had gone down on her that first time, and four more times, when, one by one, she had a Turkish Delight in her mouth as he pleasured her with his fingers.

In the morning, Ross was gone. There was a note in the bathroom, written in chocolate on the mirror.

Thank you, Leonora. I think I'd better get back to my wife now. Have a nice life, what's left of it. DR.

Clora Lynne sat on the toilet, naked, reading it. It was her turn to laugh.

Soon, she would have a shower. Then, she would call room service and get them to clean up the mess. She would leave them a very large tip. After that, went her plan, she would close up here and get on a flight to London.

Terrence Elliotte had been watching everything on her webcam, and recording it. Soon, the video would go all around the internet. At the very least, Ross would lose his marriage. She expected to see photos in the tabloids. She expected that Ross would become a laughing stock. She expected that the lump was benign. And she expected that perhaps, just perhaps, she would get her own reality show.

Half an hour later, as she stepped out of the shower and into a bathrobe, the telephone rang.

Patrick Chapman was born in 1968. He lives in Dublin. His poetry collections are *Jazztown*, *The New Pornography* and *Breaking Hearts And Traffic Lights*. He wrote the short film, *Burning The Bed*, based on the opening story in this collection. Starring Gina McKee and Aidan Gillen, the film was directed by Denis McArdle and was named 'Best Narrative Short' at the 2004 Dead Center Film Festival in Oklahoma. Another of these stories, 'A Ghost', won first prize in the 2003 *Cinescape* Genre Literary Awards. 'Happy Hour' was a finalist in the *Sunday Tribune* Hennessy Literary Awards in 1999. In 2001, he collaborated on the art exhibition and book, *The Foot Series*, with Gemma Tipton. In 2006, he co-founded the Irish Literary Revival website with Philip Casey. Chapman's bestselling audio play, *Doctor Who: Fear of the Daleks*, was released by Big Finish in 2007. It stars Wendy Padbury as Zoe and Nicholas Briggs as the Daleks.